THE JOURNEY

Stephen Simmons

Published by New Generation Publishing in 2012

First Edition

www.newgeneration-publishing.com

 New Generation Publishing

The Journey

Chapter 1

The Awareness

The warrior sat on his pony and gazed down over the valley below. Above the silence is broken by a lonely cry, it was an eagle soaring high in the sky, deer roaming among the trees, a quiet and serene peace. As he rode quietly on he was aware of a presence far beyond this place. He crossed a small ravine; babbling water over rocks, grassy verges. He stopped, dismounted and gazed into the water, fish and frogs all thriving. Water is life, his horse sipping the water, the chattering of birds, and nature at its best. He sat for what seemed ages as if he was in a trance taking in the atmosphere. The smells of the flowers, perfumes so rich it would take your breath away. He gathered his thoughts, mounted his pony and quietly rode on. By this time the light was beginning to fade. Eventually he came across a small opening by some trees and decided to stop for the night. A little further away he could hear the water from the stream. He lit a small fire and settled down for the night. He soon fell into a deep sleep only to be woken by a severe cry. He lay there gathering his thoughts. The wind whistling through the branches of the tree, the hoot of an owl and then that cry again, piercing yet it seemed a cry for help. Not moving he lay there just taking in all the night sounds. The fire was still burning brightly in the dark night air. He slipped back into a deep sleep. When he awoke daylight had broken. H e looked around he could hear the birds singing. He got up and walked towards the stream and placed his hands into the cool water, cupping them full of the cold liquid he washed his face clearing the dust from his eyes and face. His pony stood quietly grazing on the moist grass. His thoughts took him back to the severe cry he had heard in the night. He walked over to his pony and taking hold of the reigns they both walked slowly towards the opening leading into a canyon. Steep volcanic rocks either side reaching up as far as the eye could see when suddenly the pony stopped and despite all the warriors coaxing would not go any further. He let the reigns slip from his fingers and slowly walked towards a ridge of protruding rocks. As he approached the rock he was aware of something but he did not know what it was. Suddenly the peace and tranquillity was shattered by a loud growl and roar. He stopped, not knowing what he would face beyond the rocks he approached with caution. There, led on a small ledge, was the most beautiful creature he had ever seen, a beautiful white wolf. Could this be the beast he had heard that night? He walked very slowly towards the animal. The wolf was snarling, his teeth protruding in a vicious manner. The animal was magnificent. He noticed that the wolf was injured; his left hind leg had been severely bitten. Bits of flesh could be seen hanging on a large gaping wound. He had lost a lot of blood. His beautiful coat splattered with traces of blood. The warrior approached the wolf slowly taking just a few slow steps at a time until he was nearly facing him. The animal although in a considerable amount of pain seemed to know that the warrior was not a threat to him. The warrior spoke softly gazing into the wolf's deep blue eyes. The warrior raised his hand and placed it on top of the wolf's head speaking softly. The animal seemed to calm down, his ears pricked up and the growling stopped. He realised that the warrior was there to help him. Slowly the warrior ran his hand down the animals back to the injured leg. He reached into his bag for the water. Gently rubbing the water into a piece of cloth he began to clean up the animals wound. It was a large opening just behind the knuckle of the back leg. Flesh had been torn away. All the time he was talking to the wolf in a soft manner. He reached in his bag for a small needle and some catgut and proceeded to stitch the wound. The animal never flinched or cried out; he seemed to know that help was at hand. When the warrior had finished he laid mosses and herbs on top of the wound. This would make it heal more quickly. The wolf never moved. The warrior slowly rose to his feet, pouring some water into a small jug he placed the cloth into the water and began to clean away all traces of blood from the animals pure white coat, it would be a few days he thought before the wolf would be able to put any weight on the injured leg. He returned slowly to his pony and picking up the reigns they both walked slowly forward until they were just a small distance away from the wolf. The wolf did not utter a sound, his piercing blue eyes watching every move the warrior made. He slowly sat down opposite this magnificent creature and began to chant softly and once again calm and tranquillity had been restored. The warrior lit a small fire. This would keep them all warm through the night. He reached in his bag and pulled out some dried turkey meat chewing it slowly. He broke off a piece with his knife, rose slowly to his feet and approached the wolf. His eyes were piercing yet calm, the warrior held out the piece of turkey. The wolf crept forward on all fours, took the piece of meat in his jaws and retreated back never taking his eyes off the warrior who walked slowly back to the fire. As night fell all the sounds could be heard, wolves howling, owls and crickets going about their nightly chores. The warrior slept. He had no worries. He knew the wolf would still be there in the morning. Before dawn broke he was awakened by the sound of a soft cry. He slowly rose and walked over to where the wolf was lying. The animal was cold and shivering he knew he had to get some warmth into him. Grasping him with both arms he lifted him up and walked over to the fire. The wolf did not stir. He gently wrapped him in his blanket and laid him down by the fire. He put more logs on the fire and lay down by the wolf. The heat from the fire and his body heat should be enough to quell any fever. If he can get through the night the warrior knew that he would survive. Daylight broke to the sound of birds chattering. As the warrior awoke he was aware of something strange though not alarming. Thoughts of what happened in the night flashed back in his mind. As he rose to his feet he looked down, the wolf had gone, and just the blanket remained. Where could he have gone? He thought last night he was too weak to move yet this morning he had vanished without a trace. He sat for a moment just pondering his thoughts. Had he gone off somewhere to die or had he just got up and wandered off to die, or had he just got up and wandered off in a delirious state – he didn't know. After washing his face he gathered his thoughts and his belongings, put out the dying embers of the fire and walked over to his pony. He placed the blanket on the pony's back, put his bag over his shoulder and took hold of the pony's reigns. They began to walk slowly towards a grassy verge leading to a pathway winding slowly up the side of the canyon. Halfway up his thoughts were still of that magnificent animal. What happened? Where did he go? Several questions, yet no answers. Still the warrior carried on, he and his pony slowly walking a winding pathway leading out onto a vast grassy plain. The warrior mounted his pony and rode on till nightfall, eventually stopping for the night by two big oak trees near a small river. He dismounted, made a small fire and prepared to settle down for the night. The wind blew gently, the rustle of branches high in the sky. The moon illuminated the grassy plain. In the distance the cry of wolves could be heard but it was far away. As the warrior led there, his thoughts passed back to the day before when he had come across the injured wolf. A wild animal that hunted in packs, that could be so vicious yet so humble and gentle. As the fire glowed in the night, embers crackling and burning bright, he was once again in harmony with nature. Once again a new day was beginning when he woke. He walked to the river; it was only a short distance away. While washing his face he paused to gaze at his reflection in the water. So much had happened. His thoughts went back to bygone days when all his people had to worry about was finding food and the best places to set up their camps. They were good days, days of watching and teaching the young ones the ways of their people's culture. He cupped his hands again allowing the water to run down his face wiping away any trace of tears from the past. He rose to his feet and returned to his pony. He mounted and gently rode on. He had a quest searching but searching for what even he was not sure. Days went by, the seasons were changing. One afternoon he stopped at the foot of a mountain. It had started to rain. He had to find some sort of shelter. He carried on until he came across a small cave. He entered and surveyed the inside, it was empty. It had been used before but not for a long time. Remnants of a fire and an empty whiskey bottle, maybe a trapper had used it for shelter on his way up to the high country? Who knew? He made sure his trusted pony was bedded down for the night and preceded to light a small fire. While the fire gently burned he ate the dried turkey meat he had brought. The rain was still pouring down, the storm was getting worse. He wrapped himself up in his blanket and settle down for the night. Suddenly lightening illuminated the sky, it was a fierce storm. As he drifted off to sleep his mind went back to bygone days, days when he was happy playing with his son and beautiful wife. He smiled but his smile soon turned to hate as he relived that terrible day when on returning to his village he found it in ruins and the two of them dead. Bodies lay strewn around. What had happened there? He held his beautiful wife in his arms, tears falling down his face as he picked her crumpled body up in his arms. A mournful expression on his face he carried her to a burial place and laid her body on a wooden trestle supported by four wooden posts. He returned for his son and as he leant down to pick him up he noticed the bullet holes in his chest. To die so young and for nothing! Tears streamed down his face as he laid him beside his beloved mother. He prepared them both for burial. As night fell he lit the fire below the trestles and within seconds it was ablaze and engulfed in a reddish glow. He knew that their spirits had been released and had risen to a higher plane. He just sat there until nothing was left but embers and ash. He then returned to bury the rest of the dead young and old, twenty-three in total. It was hard work building the trestles. For four days he worked non stop carrying bodies to the trestles. Finally he had finished, all he had to do now was light the fires that would release their spirits. This he did and the night sky turned red, the glow could be seen for miles. The smell of burning flesh was thick in the air and by morning there were nothing left but smouldering embers. Not a lot for what once was a happy little village. He rose to his feet stricken by grief and made his way to where his pony was waiting. He mounted and started to ride away, glancing back now and again. The air was thick with the smell of death. He longed to smell the sweet fragrance of flowers or the smell of the grass after it had rained.

At that moment he was awoken by a loud roar, some kind of beast was roaming around outside the entrance to the cave. He quietly got up and slowly made his way towards the entrance and peered out. There, about ten feet away, was the biggest grizzly bear he had ever seen. The bear, obviously out searching for food, had picked up the scent of him and his pony. The warrior knew he had to do something pretty fast or they would both be killed. He returned to his pony that by now was beginning to get very restless and after running his hand over the pony's head he reached down for his rifle, which was stored in its leather pouch. He returned to the entrance to find that the bear was even closer. It started to come forward and stood on its back legs growling and snarling. The warrior had one chance he could not afford to miss. Raising his rifle he took aim. As he gently squeezed the trigger he heard a click. The rifle had jammed. He frantically tried again to pull the trigger but again nothing happened. By this time the bear was nearly on top of him and he had no choice but to draw his knife and prepared for the inevitable. Just at that moment the bear turned away, a lone creature was attracting his attention. The warrior looked on as the two animals fought it out. The bear was huge but could not move as fast as the creature fighting him. The warrior continued to look on but he could not quite make out what it was. They fought for what seemed like eternity until the bear lashed out with his giant paw swiping the creature to one side. By this time the warrior could not believe his eyes. Could this be the wolf he had helped days before? The wolf returned and the animals continued to fight until eventually the bear moved away slowly into the night. This magnificent creature had returned but why? The wolf just stood there staring at the warrior panting and crying out his growls of victory for what seemed like an eternity and then in a split second he was gone, disappearing into the night. The warrior stood motionless wondering why the wolf had returned – and why at that moment? Thoughts passed through his head. He returned to the cave and sat by the fire gazing into the burning embers. He knew deep inside that if his guardian angel had not returned when he did things could have been different.

Morning broke and the sun shone high in the sky. High above vultures circled and he knew it could only mean one thing. Something was dying or even worse already dead. He clambered down the rocky pathway which came out between two rocks. There lying on the ground was the bear, motionless, gaping wounds in his side and on his legs. He had gone off into the night and slowly bled to death because of the injuries he had received in his battle with the wolf. The warrior felt sad. Any life is sacred. We all fight for the right to survive but sometimes we lose and sadly the bear had lost his fight. The warrior started his way back, aware of the vultures gathering around the body, in this barren land nothing is wasted. He collected his pony and continued on his way wondering what lay ahead. What did the Great Spirit have in store for him next? Who knew? He rode on for two days until he could ride no more. His pony stopped and he slid of its back slowly to the ground. Feeling nothing he fell into a deep sleep. He dreamt of passed events. What was the purpose of these events? What was the message the spirits were trying to send? His mind was in turmoil and he tossed and twisted as he slept. In the morning he was awoken by bird song and the rustle of activity in the trees. His pony had wandered a short way ahead to graze. He got up and moved towards him. He reached for his water bag and proceeded to pour the water over his head in an attempt to waken himself properly. He sat cross-legged on the grass and tried to remember parts of his dream and what they could mean. He gathered his thoughts, stood up and walked over to his pony. Holding onto the pony's reigns he slowly mounted and rode quietly away the same thoughts of passed events embedded in his mind. The bear, the fight and why had the wolf returned? He did not have an answer but he knew deep inside that there was a message there somewhere. What were the spirits trying to tell him? Or show him? He was not certain. He rode on for hours. High in the sky an eagle could be heard crying. He gazed up to admire this fine hunter. The eagle circled and then dived, soaring low it circled again as if searching for something and then he pounced on a rabbit. A small cry was heard and then the eagle flew off high over the trees and hills and disappeared out of sight. The warrior sat on his pony thinking about the eagle. A mighty hunter! A symbol of truth and the emblem of his lost people. As long as the eagle flies his people's spirits would live on. He rode on and as the sun was beginning to go down he looked for somewhere to stop for the night. He noticed a grassy verge between two giant rocks, a small stream gushing with water, which came down from the mighty mountains above. He stopped, made a fire and prepared to cook a turkey which he had shot earlier that day. After he had plucked it he walked down to the stream and washed the bird, cleaning it out thoroughly. He returned to the fire piercing the bird with a stick and mounted it above the fire on two Y shaped branches which formed a kind of spit which he rotated with his hand. The fire glowed deep, the embers cracking in the silence of the night. Owls hooted, wolves howled in the distance. He cut some of the turkey and while he ate he gazed into the fire thinking of his wife and son. Tears ran down his face. His heart wrenched with pain, the memories still vivid in his mind. As he looked up at the stars he noticed a large rock jutting out from the hillside as if it was there for a reason. He rose to his feet and made his way towards it, his pathway lit by the brightness of the moon. As he approached it the rock seemed very narrow but just around this narrow section it led out onto a wide ledge. He made his way to the middle of the ledge where there was another rock, not big but rounded with a flat surface. He sat and gazed out over the valley below. The sky was bright with stars and as he looked up the moon shone and a ray of golden light lit up the ledge. He was amazed at the sight before him. He began to chant and held his hands high towards the Great Spirit. After a while, for some unknown reason, he felt a strong urge of belonging. This for him was the closest he had felt to his wife and son since they had been taken from him. He sat totally exhausted, tears flowing down his face, when he realised that he was not totally alone on the ledge. He turned slowly and there in the moonlight not five feet away was the magnificent white wolf with deep blue eyes. They looked at each other and the wolf slowly moved forward towards the warrior until he was in touching distance. As the warrior chanted the wolf howled as if in harmony with each other. Suddenly there was no doubt in the warrior's mind that the spirits had answered him. The wolf was the answer and had been sent by the spirits to assist him in his quest. As daylight approached, the warrior made his way back down to the still glowing fire, followed by the wolf. The warrior threw some branches on the embers and the flames licked around the wood and the fire blazed once again. The warrior and the wolf ate the remaining meat together. As the wolf gazed at him the warrior turned and said "White Spirit, we will travel to the ends of the earth in our quest for peace, together as one. We are the spirit's legs and body. The eagle is the spirit's eyes, seeing all and everything above and below. In the beginning there was just nature, now man destroys everything and in the end man will destroy himself. The only solution is peace and harmony, without that the world as we know it will cease to exist".

Chapter 2

The Awakening

The warrior rode slowly across the plains. After a few hours he was stopped in his tracks by the sound of gunfire. He dismounted and made his way up a slight incline. He moved slowly not making a sound. As he peered over the top he could see a group of braves, four in total. Three of them seemed to have been fighting with one young brave who was lying on the ground motionless. The warrior gasped as he saw one of the three pull his knife and walk over to the brave on the ground, the sun glinting off the blade. The warrior knew he had no time to waste. Drawing his rifle he took aim and just as the brave was about to strike with the knife a shot rang out and it flew through the air. The three startled braves looked around, astonished by this intervention. Where had the shot come from? They panicked, jumped on their ponies and rode off as fast as they could. After a short time the warrior made his way down to the injured brave who was still motionless. As he looked at him he noticed a slight wound to the side of his head, a flesh wound, but enough to render him unconscious. He was lucky, an inch either way and he could have been dead. The warrior knelt down beside the young brave and gently bathed the wound. He then placed a piece of cloth soaked in water on the young brave's forehead. After a short time the brave started to come round. The warrior made him as comfortable as he could and the young brave started to mutter something the warrior could not understand. He placed his hand on the young brave's forehead and told him to rest. The warrior had to go and fetch his pony but would return in a little while. When he returned he saw the young brave sat up in a dazed condition. He made the young brave take a swallow of water and lay back down to rest. He took his blanket and wrapped it around the brave. All he could do now was wait. Hours passed and the young brave never stirred. Just before daylight the warrior stood up and made his way down to the stream where he bathed. He dried himself off and went back to his pony. He reached into his bag and took out some dry biscuit and held some out for the pony. They had been together for a long time. He held the pony's head softly. At that time the young brave started to come round and sat upright. The warrior made his way to him and sitting down offered the young brave food and water. The young brave was full of anger and wanted revenge. The warrior, older and wiser, spoke softly but firmly to the young brave. "What you feel at the moment will pass surely as night follows day and the sun follows rain". The young brave rose to his feet still bitter over what had happened to him. "They have stolen everything" he said, "even my pony. A brave without his pony is like a bird without wings". The warrior stood up and gazed into the eyes of the young brave. "These are material things. As regards your pony, he is not the chosen one for you. When you find him your heart will tell you". The young brave did not understand. He asked the warrior how he knew this and the warrior replied, "I just know". He took his pony's reigns and proceeded to walk away. He gazed back; the young brave was just stood watching him. "Come with me" he said. The young brave hesitated and then followed him. As they walked the warrior asked the young brave "what do you see around you?" The young brave replied, "Grass, hills, trees, I hear the sounds of the birds". The warrior turned to the brave and said, "You see these living things, you hear the sounds of living creatures, you hear the wind, you see the clouds, yet you don't understand. We are here for a short time but our actions remain forever". They travelled for days; stopping at different places and eventually one afternoon they came across a small valley secluded by some big old trees, lush grass and a small stream. They stopped and made a fire and the young brave fetched the rabbits he had caught the night before. They sat beside the fire and the warrior began to tell the brave about his family and what had happened to them. The young brave's expression became taught and the warrior could see the hurt and pain in his eyes, as if he was reliving the terrible events of that night. The warrior placed his hand on the young brave's shoulder. "Do not feel sorry for me my young friend," he said. "The reason I have told you this is for you to realise we all have tragedies in our life that we have to face and share. This is what makes us stronger. Life is short; we are here for a short time only". Tears ran down the young brave's face and the warrior once again placed his hand on the brave's shoulder. "Be at peace my friend," he said, "rest now. When morning breaks we will look for Running Wind". The young brave looked at him and asked, "Who is Running Wind?" The warrior replied, "All will be revealed in the morning, rest now". As sunrise dawned the warrior rose to his feet and slowly made his way through the trees, through the clearing and out onto the grassy plain. There, about thirty feet away, stood a group of ponies grazing on the grass' morning dew. He stood silently, not moving. There were ten ponies, all mares apart from one black and white stallion that stood proud over his herd. The stallion moved to the front of the herd as if he sensed or even knew he was being watched. The warrior moved silently back behind some bushes trying not to startle the herd. The stallion moved slowly forward again and then stopped, his proud head moving up and down, his right leg pounding the ground as if he was making a stand. Suddenly he raised both front hooves in the air and let out a cry. The herd raced away down the valley until they were out of sight. It had been quite a while since the warrior had seen a sight like that. It took him back to when he was young and his father had taken him out in search of a pony. He remembered how his father had shown him the Indian ways and taught him the values of life. He always told him that everything had a purpose and to always respect nature. At that moment the warrior realised that he was not alone and turning slowly came face to face with the young brave. "Let's follow them," he said, "no" replied the warrior, "the time is not right". They both returned to where the warriors pony was grazing. Without any hesitation the young brave jumped onto the back of the warrior's pony but the pony did not move. He just stood there and raised his head round slightly to look at the young brave. The warrior just laughed as the young brave dug his heals into the side of the pony, yet still the pony did not move. The young brave, furious, slid off the pony's back and approached the warrior. "Why won't he move?" he asked the warrior who smiled and said in a soft manner "you look yet you do not see, you hear yet you do not listen. The pony is a free spirit. We have been together a long time he chooses to be with me. He will not respond to you, you want to rush away in search of the ponies. As I said before the time is not right". The young brave looked at the warrior. "When will it be right?" he asked and the warrior replied, "When the time is right you will know in your heart". The warrior took hold of the pony's reigns and slowly they walked away. The young brave followed in silence, trying to understand what the warrior had said to him. They travelled for days stopping here and there without a sighting of the ponies. It was as if they had never existed. They stopped one afternoon between a group of large trees. It was quiet, the birds were singing and the sound of water could be heard rushing over rocks. The warrior walked down to the stream to fill his water bag and wash some of the dust from his face. He gazed for a moment at his reflection in the water; his thoughts were taken back to the time when things were different and calm. When every day was a joy to be lived, it seemed so long ago. He wondered why things and events had shattered and destroyed all the values that he and his people had known. Tears ran down his face as the pictures returned in his mind of the last time he had seen his wife and son. He remembered the pain and heartbreak at returning to find their bodies lying still and motionless and death all around. At that moment he felt a hand on his shoulder. He could see the reflection of the young brave stood behind him. The young brave asked the warrior why he was sad and the warrior replied, "For a moment I was back in the past, a time of overwhelming sadness and loss. Come" he said, "let's eat". They returned in silence to the small fire the young brave had made. They both sat, not uttering a word for what seemed like hours. The young brave looked at the warrior's face. Even though he was young he could see all the pain and hurt in the warrior's eyes and facial expression. He felt at a loss, he felt helpless, what could he do? At that moment the warrior raised his head, looked at the young brave and said one word, "nothing". The young brave was amazed. How did the warrior know what he had been thinking? The warrior spoke again softly. "You have questions. All will be revealed in time. Trust in what your heart tells you. Believe in what you see and hear. We are as one. Guided by the spirits above". As darkness fell both their faces were lit up by the glow of the fire burning brightly in a blanket of darkness. At that moment the silence was broken by a twig being snapped and the rustle of bushes. The young brave stood up and the warrior said, "Do not be alarmed it is only White Spirit". The young brave sat back down unaware of what was about to happen. Slowly two bushes parted and there stood the most beautiful white wolf with deep blue eyes that the young brave had ever seen. He sat motionless, afraid to move. The warrior stood up and walked over to the wolf and placed his hand on its head. The animal never moved. The young brave could not believe what he was seeing, yet he had to believe it, the wolf and the warrior were right in front of him. The warrior and White Spirit returned to the fire. The warrior sat, raised his hands in the air and began to chant. The wolf howled in such a high pitch it sent a shiver down the young brave's back. He had never experienced anything like this before. At some part of the night the young brave had fallen into a deep sleep. When he awoke as dawn was breaking, he sat up and looked around. The warrior was still sleeping; his pony was stood a short distance away, yet there was no sign of the wolf. Did it really happen or was it a dream. The young brave sat there just thinking. The warrior awoke, turned to the young brave and said, "It was no dream. It is a sign from the spirits above. You have been chosen to carry on when my time comes to follow my destiny". The young brave said, "You mean…?" "Yes" replied the warrior. "You now see what you are looking at and hear what you are listening to and now you start learning the lessons of life. Tomorrow we go in search of your pony. This pony will carry you on your quest and will be your companion for life". That morning the sun shone high in the sky, its rich yellow colour surrounded by a bright orangey red outer. The warrior called out to the young brave, "come, look above, see how rich in colour the sun is high in the sky, it is a sign". The two of them collected their possessions and slowly walked over to the warriors pony. The young brave started to throw his blanket over the pony's back. "Stop" cried the warrior, "we carry our own possessions today, my pony needs to be free to wander. We will follow him". The warrior placed his hand on the pony's head and whispered something in his ear. His pony reacted straight away by shaking his head up and down and stamping his right hoof deep into the ground and then he was off. Just as if lightening had struck a flash and he was gone. The young brave could not believe it. He turned to the warrior and asked "why did he go and what did you say, we will never catch him now". The warrior turned to the young brave and said, "Do not be sad, come let's follow". As they walked the warrior tried to explain to the young brave what he had said to his pony and why the pony had reacted the way he did. The young brave said to the warrior, "we are both without ponies now". The warrior smiled and placed his hand on the young brave's shoulder. "Trust Me," he said, "in time all will be revealed to you. Just keep your mind open and it will be filled with knowledge, remember, before light there must be darkness and before sun there must be rain". They both walked on for some time in silence. They stopped for a drink of water from their shoulder pouches and the warrior sat down. The young brave wanted to carry on. The warrior made him sit. "Be patient" he said. The young brave asked the warrior what he was waiting for. At that moment the warrior gazed up at the blue sky and said, "You see the eagle hovering?" The young brave gazed upwards. "Watch him and tell me in which direction he circles". After some time the young brave said, "He is just circling in search of prey". The warrior pointed upward. "The eagle is a free spirit. He is showing us the way. You have to keep your mind open and believe what you see. We will follow." The eagle could be heard crying high in the sky. After about two hours they came across a small clearing with a line of tall trees in front. The warrior asked the young brave "where is the eagle now?" The young brave looked around and said, "He is gone". The warrior cupped both hands around the young brave's face and pushed it upward. "Look" he said, "believe in what you see. The eagle is above, what does that tell you?" The young brave replied, "This must be the place". The warrior said, "You now have your answer, you are now starting to listen". They moved slowly through the trees and eventually the land opened out onto a small valley with a high ridge at one end. The warrior stopped and said to the young brave, "Beyond that ridge lays your pony". The young brave's expression on his face changed. For once in his young life he was starting to learn the lessons of life. They both sat down and took a drink from their pouches. The warrior turned to the young brave and said, "We will stay here tonight and rest, tomorrow we will be fresh and able to carry out the task before us". The young brave for once did not argue. As morning broke to the song of birds, the warm glow of the sun on their faces, the warrior placed his hand on the young braves shoulder and said, "Come, the time is right". The young brave, normally full of questions, was silent. They both moved away silently through the trees and bushes towards a large grassy ledge. They both moved slowly, not a sound could be heard. When they reached the top of the ledge the warrior put his hand out to stop the young brave. He slowly turned to him and said in a soft manner, "Look below". There were about twenty ponies grazing on the lush grass. The young brave looked amazed. "How did you know they would be here?" he asked. The warrior smiled but did not utter a word. The young brave, eager to get to the ponies, dislodged a small boulder, which hurtled to the ground below and the noise was enough to startle the ponies that disappeared in a cloud of dust leaving nothing but the dust on the wind. The warrior looked at the young brave and said "Have you not learned anything?" They both made their way back in silence. The warrior sat down and took a drink. The young brave turned to the warrior full of regret and said "sorry". The warrior smiled and said "you are young, eager, you want everything now. You must learn to be patient, remember, it comes to he who waits. The eagle has to wait for the right wind currents to gain height and sore through the sky. You are young with much to learn, your life is before you, mistakes you will make but you will learn from them and be stronger for that experience". The warrior placed his hand on the young braves arm, "come" he said. They both walked down the valley listening to the sounds of the birds singing, the light breeze rustling through the branches of the trees. That night they made camp on a slope overlooking a vast forest of pine trees. As darkness fell the young brave threw some wood on the fire, its bright embers glowing red in the blackness of the night. Wolf's cries could be heard in the distance. The warrior raised his hands in the air and began to chant. The young brave just sat there in silence. The warriors chanting seemed to go on for hours and then all of a sudden he stopped. All that could be heard was the crackling of the wood on the fire. As daybreak dawned a yellow and red haze surrounded the rising sun, which slowly showered the valley below in its brightness. The warrior threw handfuls of dust onto the smouldering fire extinguishing its flame forever. He turned to the young brave and said "come, its time to move forward, destiny awaits". They moved off slowly towards the clearing between the large pine trees. They walked for hours in silence. After what seemed an eternity the young brave asked the warrior where they were going. "Be patient" he said. This went on for three days until one morning they came across a small meadow. Lush green grass, a small running river, which led down to a small ravine at one end with some, rocks just jutting out of the ground. The warrior turned to the young brave and said "this is the place. Now we sit and wait". The young brave asked "wait, wait for what?" The warrior did not answer. He gazed up at the sky. High above an eagle soared just floating gently on the wind, his wings fully stretched yet so graceful, an occasional movement of his wings as he soared higher and lower picking up the air currents. That afternoon a sight appeared on the horizon, which amazed the warrior, but completely stunned the young brave. A herd of twelve ponies were grazing. As they got closer the warrior could see his own pony grazing peacefully away from the rest of the heard. The warrior cupped his hands and murmured something the young brave did not understand. To his amazement the warriors pony started to walk towards them. Within a matter of minutes the warriors pony was stood right in front of him. The warrior embraced the pony placing his hands at the top of its head. "Welcome back my friend" he said, "you have journeyed far". After a while the warrior whispered in the pony's ear. Within seconds the pony was off leaving just a cloud of dust and disappeared into the horizon. The young brave was silent. The warrior walked over to him and placed his hand around his shoulder and said, "no words need to be spoken my young friend. What you are about to see is only for the chosen few". Shortly after, two ponies were seen on the horizon. The warrior turned to the young brave and said, "Be silent and still. What ever happens now, do not move". Within minutes a large cloud of dust came up over the horizon completely covering the two ponies. The sound of hooves could be heard thundering across the ground, the dust cloud moving closer until it covered everything in its path. The young brave covered his eyes. It seemed as though he was stood right in the middle of a stampeding herd. He remembered what the warrior had told him and did not move. He stood there for what seemed an eternity. Eventually he took his hands away from his face and opened his eyes. The dust started to clear very slowly. In the distance he could see two outlines but the dust cloud was still too dense to make out exactly what it was. Eventually the dust moved slowly away leaving a sight before him which even he could not imagine. There before his very own eyes stood two ponies, one he knew, the other he did not. Frightened to move he just stood silently. The warrior, who was stood not far away, walked over to the young brave and said, "Do not be alarmed, the sight you have just seen is granted to only the chosen few". The young brave could not utter a word. The warrior said to the young brave "take my hand and walk very slowly" and led him over to where the two ponies were standing. Silently he turned to the young brave and said "do exactly what I do". The warrior placed his hands on his pony's head and the young brave did the same to his pony but as he did the pony moved backwards just a short distance and stopped. The warrior said to the young brave "This time when you place your hand on his head do it with the feelings you have in your heart. If you do it right he will not move". The young brave placed his hand once more on the pony's head. This time the pony did not move proving to the young brave the trust between man and beast.

Chapter 3

The Challenge of Life

The warrior spoke softly to the young brave teaching him the knowledge he would need to be as one with his pony, Running Wind. He told him it would take patience, feeling and understanding and all the love that he had in his heart. The young brave asked the warrior how long would it take to acquire all of these things and the warrior replied, "It will take you a life time. I will help you as much as I can but some of these things you will have to learn yourself". The young brave reached into his bag and pulled out a length of rope. He started to make a loop in the rope and place it over his pony's nose. The pony moved backwards. The warrior picked up the rope and threw it high in the air. The young brave asked the warrior why he had thrown the rope in the air and he replied, "Running Wind chose you! What gives you the right to place a rope around his nose? He is a free spirit and as such must never be tied or roped in any way". The young brave asked the warrior "How am I supposed to lead him then?" The warrior replied, "Lead him? Running Wind will lead you! He will be your companion for life all you need to do is trust him. Many moons ago I told you that the spirits had chosen you. When my time comes to seek my destiny Running Wind will carry you on your quest through life's journey. The things I teach you now will keep you safe and make you stronger. Always remember you are not alone. If you seek knowledge then raise your eyes to the blue skies, the eagle above will give you the answers you seek and at night when you are sat by the fire do not fear for White Spirit is with you. If you call he will come, he will give you strength, courage and stamina for what lies ahead. The journey you are about to undertake will take you in your forefather's footsteps. The spirits above are your light when all around you is darkness. The visions you will see will be an insight into the past, the sufferings and pain your people had to endure. All these things you will see, you will feel the pain and you will feel the suffering and most of all you will feel what death is like. But what ever confronts you remember my words to you, never feel afraid for you are chosen and you are protected by a power so huge it will be beyond your wildest dreams". That night they both sat by the fire, the glowing red embers lighting up a reddish flame in the blackness of the night. The young brave asked the warrior how he had acquired his powers. The warrior replied "they are not acquired they are given. When I returned to my village many moons ago the sight which met my eyes was frightening. Death was all around. You could see it and smell it in the air. Young braves lying dead on the ground; they had fallen trying to protect their wives and children. My own wife and son lying together on the ground lifeless". The young brave asked, "Did you not feel anger, did you not want revenge?" The warrior replied, "I felt all of these things but after days of nothing but burial fires the fight in you is gone. My heart felt heavy with sadness and pain. It was at that time when all the burials had been completed that I sat down to rest. The sun was just starting to go down, the brightness of the day being replaced with a dark blanket of cloud which seemed to cover the entire sky. I can remember looking up at the darkness, tears streaming down my face, wondering why all of my people had been killed. What was the purpose? What did they achieve by these killings? It was at that time the moon started to appear high in the sky separating two big masses of black darkness. I raised both my arms high towards the sky. With tears still running down my face I asked the great spirits for help and guidance. I closed my eyes and waited, it was not long. First I heard the beating of drums then I heard the wind blowing through the trees, then the drumbeats started to get louder. I do not know if I was awake or asleep but what I know is from that point my life changed. Thunder and lightening cracked across the open sky. It was at this moment I opened my eyes. The sky was lit up, white light flashing across a blue haze surrounded by small flashes of what looked like fire. In the sky the colours were truly amazing. Within seconds the drumbeats got slower and the thunder and lightening stopped. There was a calmness in the air. What happened next was also truly amazing. Right in front of my eyes twenty braves appeared on ponies riding across the night sky. All the braves and ponies were lit up with a bright white light and a blue haze of light surrounded every brave and pony. I could hear and see with my own eyes the thundering of hooves yet no dust was kicked up. After a while the braves and ponies stopped. They moved into two lines of ten and a white path of fluffy cloud seemed to form some sort of pathway. The drumbeats started to get stronger yet not loud. The sight which appeared before my eyes next was beyond belief. I could see a number of figures between the two lines of ponies and as they got loser I could see a woman holding a child in her arms. It was my wife and son. I jumped to my feet. A part of me wanted to run towards them but I could not move, it was as if my feet were rooted to the ground and I was unable to move. All the figures moved towards me slowly until they were in front of me. I reached out to touch my wife and child but my hand seemed to glide right through them. This left me feeling empty and alone. Then the light became brighter, I had to shield my eyes from the brightness. A lone figure walked slowly towards me, he was surrounded by a white light but around his head and shoulders the light was blue. He held both his hands out towards me. For a moment I did nothing, then he spoke, he told me that I must look forward and not live in the past. I held out my hands expecting it to be like the experience with my wife and son but to my amazement it was not. He held my hands tightly in a firm grip and told me to follow. It was truly an amazing time. I walked through the line of ponies as if I was floating on air. At the end of the line of ponies stood six old chiefs dressed in full headdress. They each greeted me, placing their hands on my head and chanting. I had never been to a place so calm and peaceful. Behind the chiefs stood rows and rows of young men, women and children. The figure who had led me to this place turned towards me. Until now I had not seen his face, it had been hidden by the bright light, he was very old, the lines in his face were deep, battled scars could be seen on both sides of his face yet his eyes were a deep brown hazelnut colour. He spoke softly yet stern, but his manner was always calm. He told me that what had happened to my people had happened to the Indian nation for a very long time. He told me it was a time of change, a time of new beginnings and for me it was a time to trust. He held my hands tightly and told me I had been chosen by the high spirit council to show the Indian nation the way. The visions I was show have appeared to me in one way or another. He told me that I would come across a young brave who would need my help and who would carry on after I have left this earth plain. As we were walking back through the lines of ponies I asked the old chief if I was dreaming all of this and how could I feel his hands yet I could not feel my own wife and child. He stopped and told me to hold out both my hands, which I did. They were gripped tightly as the white cloud thinned out and there in front of me were my wife and son. Tears flowed from all our eyes and she spoke to me saying, "Do not worry for we are all safe here". I gripped her hand and my son's, I did not want to leave them but I knew I had to. Her last words to me were "Do not worry, I will always be here waiting for you" and that was the last thing that I remember. These things I say to you, trust in your heart, trust in the spirits, for they will never let you down". The young brave just sat there silently, not uttering a word, but the warrior noticed tears were slowly running down the young brave's face. He placed his hand on his shoulder, "take comfort from me" he said. "This is what life is all about. The suffering, the pain and most of all losing the ones you love. But in time you will come to terms with all of these feelings, until then rest for we have much to do tomorrow". The night passed quickly and daybreak dawned but this would be a day like no other. The warrior awoke and walked slowly down to the river to bathe. As he washed his face he could see his reflection in the water and his mind was cast back to the night before and all the things he had talked about to the young brave. The warrior knew that the young brave was the right person to carry on when it was his time to depart this earth. For the warrior had seen the tears in the young brave's eyes and felt the love in his heart. The warrior knew the great spirits had chosen well. At that moment the warrior felt a presence and knew it was the young brave because he could see his reflection in the water. The warrior turned to the young brave and said, "Come my friend, let's start our journey together through life's troubled pathways". They both walked slowly back to where they had spent the night. The young brave made sure the fire was completely out and both picked up their water bags and blankets and walked over to their ponies. The warrior turned to the young brave and said, "Always remember what I have told you" and the young brave replied, "I will never forget!" He placed his blanket on Running Wind's back and the pony moved its head round to the side and looked at the young brave. The warrior smiled and said to the young brave, "He is waiting for you to climb on his back". The young brave seemed hesitant, the warrior spoke to him again softly, "Faith my friend". The young brave mounted his pony and slowly they both made their way out onto the vast grassy plains. It was a beautiful bright sunny day, the sun shone high in the sky it's warmth beaming down. White fluffy clouds seemed to float motionless in the blue sky. A light breeze rustled through the tall grasses. A little way ahead buffalo could be seen grazing. The warrior turned to the young brave and said, "Look my friend, that is a sight I remember well. When I was young I could remember vast herds of buffalo covering these grassy plains and now these herds are much smaller. They have been hunted to near extinction by the white man who killed these beasts, not for food, but for the hides which they sold. Massive herds were slaughtered. These plains and many like them ran red with the blood of these beasts. The young brave asked the warrior why these animals had been slaughtered and the warrior replied, "The Indian kills only what he needs to survive. He eats the meat, the hide is used for making clothes and moccasins, nothing is wasted. The white man kills only for greed. He skins the animal, takes the hide and leaves the carcases to rot. Massive herds of buffalo have been wiped out in this way. The Indian could always rely upon the buffalo for food, but since the white man came the buffalo have gone. I have seen Indian villages starving, no buffalo to hunt, children reduced to eating rabbit or prairie dog. Whole villages having to move in their search for food. I cannot forget the sight of old people and children dying through starvation. There were days when the only things they could find to eat were roots and berries and at times when things were really bad they had to eat their ponies. I've seen whole villages fighting amongst themselves over a wild turkey. These were bad times and very sad times. The Indian nation is proud. The Indian lives in harmony with nature. This balance has been upset by the white man's greed and his lust for killing. The day will come when the white man will pay the ultimate price for his actions on this earth. Mother Nature grows stronger by the day and in time she will destroy the white man with her ultimate power". Tears ran down the young brave's face as he said to the warrior, "what can we do to change this? We are only two people" and the warrior replied, "We may only be two people but always remember it only takes one to make a difference. You have been chosen to show our people the way forward. It will not be easy but you will be guided by the great spirits above and protected from harm. Your life has already been mapped out for you, everything you do, every action you take, every decision you make has been foreseen". The young brave stopped his pony and asked the warrior, "Why me, why have I been chosen, what is so special about me?" The warrior smiled and answered "You are young, strong, spirited. You were chosen when you were still in your mother's womb. You will be a leader of people and eventually a warrior of life, you carry all the hopes and dreams of the Indian nation, you were born to set the balance of nature right. This will not be an easy task but you will achieve it before your time comes to join the Great Spirit council above". For once the young brave was silent. By now it was late afternoon and the warrior suggested they found somewhere to stop for the night. They rode on for another hour and eventually came across an embankment leading down to a small stream surrounded by three old trees which stood tall and proud, their branches reaching out as if grasping the wide open spaces. The warrior said to the young brave, "This is a special place, a spiritual place. Look at the tall trees, see how they stand tall and proud with their branches reaching out to life itself!" The young brave looked at the trees and said, "They have been here a long time". The warrior replied "These trees have stood in this place for over one hundred and fifty years, they have witnessed many things". The young brave was silent and the warrior turned to him and spoke. "I am surprised, this is the first time you have not had a question. Usually when I have said something to you, you ask me why or how do I know"? The young brave looked at the warrior with a blank expression yet his eyes looked crystal clear. He said, "It's this place. There is something about this place. I do not know what it is but there is a presence of which I cannot explain". The warrior smiled, placed his hand on the young brave's shoulder and said, "Welcome my friend. Now you are starting to learn. Go collect some wood and start a fire as it is going to be cold tonight". As the darkness fell they sat round the fire talking. The fire glowed bright in the darkness, the embers cracking, little bits of wood floating upwards toward the sky being carried on the wind. The warrior placed his blanket around his shoulders and put his hands out to warm them. The young brave said to the warrior, "This place is so quiet yet alive". The warrior turned to him and said, "Before this night is over you will have learnt some of the ways of your forefathers. Remember, seeing is believing. Always go with what is in your heart". The young brave placed more wood on the fire and the flames grew brighter as they lapped the wood.

They both moved back a little from the fire as they felt the heat coming from it. They carried on talking and the young brave asked the warrior how he had known where to find him. The warrior said, "Three days before I found you I had a vision telling me where to find you and what to do. These things I now tell you". The young brave asked what he meant by a vision. The warrior replied, "Rather than tell you I will show you". He raised both his hands in the air and began to chant. Within a short time a grey mist appeared in front of the trees and in a split second the mist turned into White Spirit. The beautiful wolf with deep blue eyes walked over to the warrior and sat beside him. The young brave was amazed. As the warrior read the young brave's thoughts he said to him, "You can do this. Just believe in yourself and trust in what your heart tells you". The young brave placed both his hands in the air and began to chant and once again the grey mist appeared in front of the trees. The young brave remained seated to the spot unable to move. He just kept staring into the grey mist, which seemed to float upwards. Then, without any warning a figure like silhouette stepped forward. The young brave could see it was a very old Indian chief dressed in full Indian headdress, the feathers long and colourful and stretched right down both sides of his body nearly touching the floor. The figure walked slowly towards the young brave until he was just in front of him. The young brave just sat there. He was unable to move yet he was aware of what was in front of him. Never before in his young life had he experienced anything like this. His young eyes transfixed on the figure in front of him. The old chief spoke to the young brave in a stern yet mild manner. "You have been chosen by the Spirit Council to lead the Indian nation away from all the killings and starvation brought about by the white man. To lead the

Indian people to a brighter future, back to the old ways, back to the days when the Indian was in perfect harmony with nature. Raise your eyes to the dark sky above. In all its blackness the moon shines brightly, shedding light across the land giving hope of another day dawning". The young brave asked the old chief why he had been chosen for this task and he replied, "You were chosen many moons ago to lead our people to a better way of life. A life full of happiness, full of hopes and dreams, not as it is now full of destruction and death. Our people have been led in the wrong way by the white man full of greed and hate. It will be your task on this earth to lead our people and show them the path to a more fulfilling life. It will not be easy. You are young, strong and eager. You will encounter many problems on your journey but always remember I will always be on hand to help you and guide you through. At the moment you have the warrior, listen to him; you have much to learn from him. Remember he can show you all the things you will need to know to complete your task. As daybreak dawns remember the things I have told you, gaze upward toward the sky, I will send you a message, a sign of hope. Remember, look and you will find". The old chief moved slowly back into the grey mist which gently moved upwards until it was totally gone. The young brave turned to the warrior and said, "That was a sight which I will never forget and will always remember". Dawn was starting to break, the sun rising slowly out of the blackness of the night, but this would be no ordinary day. By the end of this day a new beginning would be born. As the warrior put out the last remaining embers of the fire he turned to the young brave and said, "Remember what the old chief said to you, look for the sign!" By now the sun was shining brightly, its golden rays warming the earth below. They both mounted their ponies and slowly moved forward heading between two canyons following what looked like a very old well-trodden trail. The young brave kept looking all around him. The warrior said to the young brave, "Cast your mind back to what the old chief said to you. Gaze upwards, not around". The young brave gazed upwards and after about an hour he said to the warrior, "All I see is two big rocks either side of this trail we are on". The warrior replied, "Be patient my young friend, you have been told the sign will come". Shortly after the young brave shouted, "Up there!" There high in the sky were two eagles circling. They seemed to just float motionless on the air currents, their huge wings hardly moving. The warrior said to the young brave, "There is your sign my young friend. They have been sent to you for a reason". They proceeded further into the canyon which narrowed and then opened out onto a grassy plain with trees along one side. The young brave looked up; the sun's heat by now was blazing down. He was finding it difficult to look upward as the sun's brightness was making his eyes water. The warrior said, "Only look upward when you have partial cover from the rocks. Then you will not feel the sun's burning rays in your eyes". Under cover of a piece of pointed rock the young brave gazed upward but the eagles were gone. The young brave turned to the warrior and said, "The sky is empty, the eagles are not there" and the warrior replied, "Those birds carry the knowledge, they are free spirits, that is the message". Shortly afterward the young brave spotted four vultures circling high in the sky. He turned to the warrior and said, "Look, this can mean only one thing, death". The warrior replied, "Every living thing has its purpose, these birds are the cleaners of life, they dispose of the carcases left on the earth, even they have a purpose. Every living thing has a reason for living but the day always arrives when it is time to die and to make way for new life". It was another hour before they arrived at the place where the vultures were circling and as they gazed down the canyon they could see a pony stood very still. It had been pulling some kind of wooden stretcher and upon it laid a figure. Without a moments hesitation they made their way down to where the pony stood. As they approached it the pony moved slightly backward. The warrior dismounted and walked over to the pony whispering to it and stroking its head. This seemed to have a calming effect on the animal so the warrior proceeded to the wooden stretcher. Upon this was led a very old woman, her face all wrinkled and blistered by the sun's constant heat. He asked the young brave to bring him his water bag and poured water on his fingers and moistened the old woman's lips. He then moistened a piece of cloth and placed it on her forehead. She was muttering something but the warrior was unable to make out what she was trying to say. They moved her a short distance away into the shade of some rocks. The warrior told the young brave that she had come here to die and the young brave asked him why she had not stayed with her own people. The warrior replied, "Pride my friend. She wanted to be alone to die, alone to find her destiny. This is a very old and proud woman, all we can do now is make her comfortable and make her last hours on this earth peaceful". He asked the young brave to make a fire while he set about making the burial table. The warrior was gone for a few hours and when he returned he told the young brave that he had selected a place half way up the canyon where there was a ledge that faced out towards the sky. He said that everything was ready for when the time came for the old woman to pass over to the great spirits. That night they took it in turns to watch over her. The warrior told the young brave that she would not see the dawn break. As the warrior sat gazing up at the stars he saw one shining brighter than the rest and suddenly it shot across the blackness of the sky. He turned and said to the young brave, "Her time has come". He lent over the old woman, she was motionless and still, "She has gone," he said. Picking her up in his arms he started to walk up the canyon to where he had prepared the burial table and placing her small and frail body on the table he then wrapped her blanket around her and closed her eyes with his right hand. "She is ready now for her spirit to be released," he said. He began to chant as he lit the burial fire and it was not long before the flames had engulfed the completed burial site, flames shooting high in the sky completely illuminating the area around the ledge and glowing bright in the darkness. The warrior and the young brave just sat there motionless and very still, the only sound to be heard was the crackling of the wood as small embers floated upwards glowing bright in the darkness. As dawn broke the ledge was covered with wood ash, which was being blown away by the wind. The warrior said to the young brave, "Within a short time this ledge will be completely cleansed by nature's wind, scattering these ashes across this land". As they made their way back to their camp below they could see that their fire was nearly out and the warrior kicked some dust over it putting it out completely. He then went over to his pony and placed his blanket on its back. The young brave asked the warrior "Where is the old woman's pony? The only thing here is the wooden stretcher lying on the ground". The warrior replied, "The pony was her means of getting to this place, he has gone for she has no more need of him now". That night they made camp between two high peaks of the canyon. They both sat down by the fire. As darkness fell the night sky was illuminated by a full moon, casting long shadows of the two tall peaks across the canyon floor. Stars shone bright in the sky, twinkling their brightness individually. They sat silent, just the sound of the wood burning and crackling on the fire could be heard. The young brave turned to the warrior and started to tell him about his past, how he and his parents had been told to leave their village. The warrior just looked at the young brave but said nothing. He told the warrior he and his mother and father had been told to leave the village because he would not fight against the white man. He was branded a coward by all the other young braves of his village. He said that he felt guilty for both his parents were old and frail and that he felt responsible for their deaths. The warrior placed his hand on his shoulder and said, "You were not responsible for the death of your mother and father. It was their time to move to a higher place, a new spiritual beginning. They are happy now and at peace and are pleased to see the way in which you are developing into a spiritual force. Also they were very proud of you for not retaliating when the other braves were taunting you because you would not fight. All these qualities were instilled in you when you were still in your mother's womb. These things you have told me I already knew". The young brave just sat there, silent and wide-eyed, amazed at what the warrior was telling him. The warrior went on to tell him that the night he released his wife and son's spirits he had had a visit from a very old spirit chief who had told him that his path would cross with a young brave who, in time and with guidance, would become a true spiritual leader of the Indian nation. The warrior told the young brave, "Close your eyes and think of your mother and father". The night was still, the only noise the sound of the wood crackling on the fire, the glow of the fire reflecting in both their faces. They started to chant, their hands held out, palms upward and after a short time a blue mist started to appear in front of them. It seemed to wash over them. They continued to chant and at that moment two figures started to appear, one was an old Indian man holding the hand of an old Indian woman. Both figures walked slowly toward the young brave and the old woman held out her arms. The young brave stood up and walked towards her, they both embraced. The same happened with the old man. The three of them returned to the fire and sat down. The young brave had so many questions! His mother spoke softly and placing her hand on his lips she said, "Be silent my son, listen to what your father and I have to say for we have so little time". They spoke to him of all the things that had happened in the past and of all the things that were going to happen in the future. They both told him how very proud of him they were. Tears ran down the face of the young brave. His mother held his hand and said to him, "Do not be sad my son for one day we will all be together for ever, but until then you must carry on. All the hopes and dreams of the Indian nation lie upon your shoulders. This we know is a heavy burden but you are the one who has been chosen by the Great Spirit Council and we have come to you tonight to give you strength and courage for the task ahead". They turned to the warrior and thanked him for all that he had done for their son. The warrior replied that no thanks were necessary. The old man and woman stood up, said their farewells and walked slowly away from the fire and disappeared into the blue mist. The young brave, silent but with tears still running down his face, turned to the warrior and said, "That was the most beautiful and fulfilling experience I have ever felt. To see my mother and father again was a sight that will live with me forever". The warrior told him, "Believe in your heart, see the picture in your

41

mind and it will appear before your eyes". He placed his hand on the young braves shoulder and told him to rest as it would soon be daylight. Dawn broke to the sound of birds singing. As the sun started to rise, its rich yellow glow surrounded by deep blue sky and white soft clouds, an eagle soared high in the sky, its call could be heard carried on the wind for miles. The warrior told the young brave that the eagle had come to show them the way. They cleared away their belongings, put out the last dying embers of the fire and made their way over to where their ponies were grazing. They placed their blankets over their pony's backs, picked up the reigns and walked out towards the vast grassy plain. The young brave looked at the warrior and said, "Today I feel is a new beginning, a new start. The feeling I feel now is something I have never felt before". The warrior smiled and said, "I know this feeling you speak of, I have felt it. This feeling takes over your whole being. It's a feeling of fulfilment and love for your fellow human beings. You have learned well, remember your loved ones are always with you in times of need". They mounted their ponies and gently rode across the open plain for hours and as the light began to fade they made camp near a big old oak tree standing alone surrounded by grassy banks on either side. As they settled down for the night the sound of wolf's cries could be heard in the distance carried by the wind. They sat talking about the past and the young brave said to the warrior, "We have been together quite a while now and I do not even know your name". The warrior replied, "Names my friend are not important, it's the things that you do with your life that matter and the things you achieve. These are the things people remember you for". As the night went on rain started to fall and they both reached for their blankets. Thankfully it did not rain for long and they soon dried out by the fire then slept. As morning broke they were awoken by the sound of gunfire in the distance. They both ran towards their ponies, mounted them and rode off towards the direction of the gunfire. They had been riding for about half an hour when they came across a wagon on fire and two bodies lying on the ground. The warrior dismounted and walked over to one of the bodies, it was a young woman. She had been raped and killed. Alongside her lay a young man who had been shot repeatedly. The warrior turned to the young brave and said, "This is a complete waste of life. Savages are what we are called by the white man, after seeing these two young bodies I can understand why". The warrior covered the young woman with some clothes that were scattered around and he asked the young brave to look around for a shovel. He picked up her frail and lifeless body and walked over to a bank where a few wild prairie flowers were growing. He gently laid her body on the ground then went back and picked up the young man. He brought him to where he had laid the young woman and placed him beside her. "This place will do," he said and the young brave started to dig. They took it in turns to dig and after about an hour it was ready for the two bodies to be placed in. They laid them side-by-side, filled in the grave and put some stones around it. The young brave asked the warrior why they have buried them and the warrior replied, "The white man may not have our ways or beliefs but *all* human life deserves respect. At that moment the cry of an eagle could be clearly heard. The warrior gazed up. A magnificent bird kept circling high in the sky. He turned to the young brave and said, "He is warning us of danger approaching". A few moments later the warrior's eyes were drawn to a hill just a short distance away. He could see six riders on ponies. The eagle kept circling and calling out his distinctive cry. One of the riders picked up his rifle and fired at the eagle but it was too high and out of range. The warrior's face frowned with anger. He ran towards his pony and the young brave followed. Both of them rode towards the six Indian braves who started to shout and yell and race down towards them. Bullets fired by the six braves flew past the warrior's head and within seconds he fired off at least half a dozen shots. Four of the Indian braves fell from their ponies. The two remaining braves fled over the hill. It was a sight truly amazing, one which the young brave would never forget. The warrior stopped by one of the dead braves. He slipped off his pony's back and walked over to the brave lying on the floor, his face painted with red and white paint, two lines on his cheeks. He said to the young brave, "Look, these are renegades. All they do is rape and kill. These are bad examples of the Indian people. This element of hatred and greed must be stamped out". The young brave slid off his pony and looked at the young Indian lying motionless on the ground. He turned to the warrior and said, "He is about my age, so young". The warrior said, "Do not feel sorry for him or the others, they chose this way to live. They never showed any mercy to that young woman or man we just buried and if they had their way we would be lying dead as well". The young brave started to lift the dead brave from the ground. "What are you doing?" the warrior asked. "We cannot leave them here, they deserve to have their spirits released" the young brave answered. "Leave them where they fell, they deserve nothing. They would not be allowed to enter the Great Spirit's world. They have brought shame on us. Leave them for the prairie dogs and vultures; at least they will serve some purpose". The young brave looked horrified; he just stared at the warrior, unable to speak. The warrior mounted his pony and started to ride away. The young brave stood there for a while not knowing what to do, then he mounted his pony and followed. They rode together in total silence, the young brave trying to come to terms with the past events. As darkness began to fall they stopped and made camp for the night. Still in total silence the young brave gathered wood and started a fire. They both sat down and had something to eat and drink. As the fire burned brightly the reflections of the flames lit up their faces. The warrior turned to the young brave and said, "Today I did something I am not proud of. I killed four of my own people. This goes against all my principles. Life is sacred. I will answer for my actions when my turn comes to rise to the Spirit World". The young brave said, "You have taught me many things. We have been together a long time. Please forgive me for doubting you earlier today but I could not understand why you and I buried the two white people but left the four renegades lying where they fell. But now I understand why, the white people never had a choice but the renegades did". The warrior looked at the young brave and said, "You have a wise head on young shoulders. You will have to make tough decisions, ones you will not like, but they must be done. As time goes by you must learn to live with them. I regret killing those four young men today but if I had not we would be dead and they would just go on killing across the land. Remember, aggression will always catch up with the aggressors. We are all accountable for our actions and we all pay the ultimate price. Death comes in many ways, quiet, swift and slow. The way we die is already mapped out before we are born". The young brave looked at the warrior's face. His eyes watering, his silver hair shining, these were things he had not really noticed before. They had been together quite a while but this was the first time he realised that the warrior was getting old. He placed his blanket around the warrior's shoulders. The warrior smiled but said nothing; the young brave said nothing but felt sad inside. He just had this feeling that the warrior would not be around for much longer. This gave him an overwhelming feeling of loss. At that moment the warrior placed his hand on the young brave's shoulder and said, "Do not worry my young friend for we will never be parted, now rest for we have a long day tomorrow". The young brave placed more wood on the fire and as the wood crackled with the heat, the flames licking the new wood, glowing embers rising slowly in the darkness, he just sat gazing into the depths of the fire. The warrior slept moving slowly in his sleep and the young brave watched him in case he moved too close to the fire. He was muttering something in his sleep but the young brave could not understand what he was saying. He lifted the blanket and placed it around the warrior. After a while the only sound to be heard was the fire burning and the sound of wolf's cries in the distance. The young brave looked up at the night sky, totally black apart from two silvery stars twinkling brightly in a blanket of darkness. He then led down and went to sleep.

The following morning started the same as usual yet there was something different. The sun was shining brightly in the sky, birds were singing, a light wind rustled through the branches of the trees, yet there was calmness, a feeling of peace. The warrior awoke and took a drink from his water bag, splashing some on his face. He looked at the young brave sleeping. He stood up and walked silently, not wishing to wake him, over to his pony. He placed some water in a small bowl and the pony started to drink. He placed his hand on the pony's head and whispered to him, "Our journey is coming to an end my faithful friend. We have travelled many pathways and we have both seen many things".

As the warrior gazed into the pony's eyes he could see flashes of the past. As the tears ran down the warriors face the pony pushed his arm with his head. The warrior smiled and placed his arm around the pony's neck, kissing him on his head and whispered in his ear, "Thank you my trusted friend, you always make me feel better". At that moment the young brave awoke. He rubbed his eyes and asked the warrior if he was all right and the warrior replied, "Everything is calm and peaceful". The young brave thought about the feeling he had last night about the warrior. He was about to mention it when the warrior said to him, "Funny things dreams, sometimes you remember them other times you do not". This made the young brave think "Was I awake or did I dream it?" He looked at the warrior who looked back at him and smiled. "Come" he said, "Let's be on our way". As they both mounted their ponies and rode away towards the canyon in the distance, the young brave had a strange feeling that this day would be like no other yet it seemed the same. As they rode they talked about many things, at times laughing about things that had happened in the past. To the young brave it seemed just like old times, he completely forgot about the feelings he had had the night before. The warrior said to the young brave, "See those two tall peaks of rock standing straight and proud? Beyond there is a valley with crystal water and the greenest grassland you have ever seen. Tonight we will camp there". As they got closer to the canyon the warrior slowed up looking around and gazing up. The young brave was also aware, he knew something was not right; for one thing it was quiet which was unusual, no birds, no sound, just silence. The warrior stopped and got off his pony and the young brave asked him what was wrong. The warrior replied, "It's too quiet, I sense danger ahead, keep your eyes open and expect the unexpected". As they started to go through the canyon the warrior's pony stopped and reared up on its back legs. The warrior held onto its reigns and gently calmed him down. He said to the young brave, "See, he senses it as well". As they carried on parts of the canyon got narrower and parts got wider and eventually they could see the opening in the distance. The warrior said to the young brave, "Just past that opening lays the valley". At that moment a haunting cry could be heard, it echoed all round the canyon walls. They both stopped, looked up and all around but could not see anything. The young brave asked the warrior what animal had made that sound and the warrior replied, "That was no animal. The sound we heard was man made". Shortly afterwards a shot rang out, the bullet missing the warrior by inches, its sound echoing round the canyon walls. They both got down behind a big rock and the young brave asked the warrior if he could see who had fired the shot. The warrior replied, "I can see two figures high up on a ledge". "Who are they" the young brave asked "and why are they firing at us?" The warrior replied, "they are the two renegades who fled when their band were killed. They ran away and now they seek vengeance. They hide like cowards afraid to show their faces". The warrior reached for his rifle and told the young brave to stay down behind the rock. The young brave wanted to go with the warrior but he said, "Wait for me, I will return". The warrior slipped silently away not making a sound, it seemed like eternity for the young brave, over an hour had passed when suddenly a single shot rang out. The young brave raised his head to see a figure falling to the ground. His heart pounded as he raced towards the figure lying face down on the canyon floor. As he reached the body he realised it was not the warrior and he cried out a sigh of relief. Looking up he could not see anyone then he heard the voice of the warrior from high up on a ledge telling him to go back to the rock and stay there. Just at that moment he saw the warrior lean forward and as he turned he could see an arrow sticking out of the warriors back. The young brave raced up the canyon wall towards the warrior and as he approached the ledge he could see the warrior leaning up against the canyon wall, the arrow still visible, blood pouring from the wound. As the young brave got closer he could see the warriors rifle lying on the ground, he picked it up just as the last renegade was about to attack the warrior with a knife. The young brave had no hesitation, he fired the rifle hitting the renegade who slipped over the edge and landed dead on the canyon floor. The young brave ran towards the warrior who was now lying on his side on the ground. He took off his coat and rolled it up and rested the warrior's head on it. The warrior asked the young brave to remove the arrow but the young brave replied, "I don't know how". The warrior said, "Listen to me. Give me something to bite on and when I say, gently pull the arrow out". The young brave looked around and found a small piece of branch, stripped of the dead bark and gave it to the warrior. "That will do fine" he said, placed it in his mouth and bit down hard. He looked at the young brave and nodded. The young brave gripped the stem of the arrow and pulled it out. As the point of the arrow left the warrior's body he bit so hard on the piece of wood that it snapped and at that point he passed out. The young brave ran back down the canyon to get a blanket and his water bag. When he returned the warrior was lying motionless and the young brave, tears running down his face, knelt down beside him. He could still hear him breathing and pulled up his shirt to reveal a hole where the arrow had entered the warrior's body. He bathed the wound, cleaned it up and covered it with herbs and mosses then bound it with some strips of clothing he had ripped up. He wrapped the warrior in the blanket then made a fire. By this time it was starting to get dark. All he could do now was wait. He prayed to the spirits for guidance. The warrior was mumbling something but the young brave could not understand. He kept bathing the warrior's forehead with a damp piece of cloth trying to keep his fever down. The warrior started to shiver so the young brave put more wood on the fire and then led down beside him hoping the heat from the fire plus his body heat would be enough to break the fever. Only time would tell, the next few hours would be crucial. That night seemed never ending and the young brave never slept at all. Every time the warrior moved or muttered he was on hand to help him in any way he could, always hoping the fever would break. He kept bathing his forehead trying to bring his temperature down but the warrior never moved. The young brave sat by the fire praying to the spirits for help. He gazed at the arrow lying on the ground. He stood up and walked over and picked it up, tears running down his face. He looked at the slender piece of wood wondering how something so slim had the ability to kill. He held it in both hands and snapped it into two pieces and threw them onto the fire. By this time dawn was starting to break and as he sat by the warrior he thought, "If only I had not taken his attention maybe he would not have been hit by the arrow". He felt guilty. He kept thinking that it was his fault that the warrior was laying motionless. He was filled with guilt. He moved the warrior onto his front to inspect the wound but there was no change. He put more mosses and herbs onto the wound and fresh cloth to keep it clean. All that day he never left the warrior's side. Daylight came and went. Darkness again began to fall and that night he felt so alone. With the fire burning bright and tears flowing down the young brave's face he gazed up at the stars shining brightly in the darkness. He could hear distant wolf cries and wondered why White Spirit had not been there in the warrior's hour of need. His heart felt heavy. For two days and nights he never slept but still the warrior did not move. Every day he attended to his wound and moistened his lips with water. On the third night, from sheer exhaustion, he fell into a deep sleep but before daylight he was awoken by a wolf's howl, so loud yet so gentle, he sat up but could see nothing but he could feel some kind of presence as he drifted back to sleep. When he awoke in the morning he looked at the warrior. He seemed to have a peaceful expression upon his face. The young brave wondered if he had dreamt about the wolf or if he had really heard it. As he put more wood on the fire he sat down and took a drink. He looked at the warrior who seemed to have a bit of colour in his face. He hoped that this was the fever breaking and not the heat from the fire. As he glanced back, to his amazement standing right in front of him was White Spirit with his beautiful white coat and deep blue piercing eyes. He raised his head and let out one long howl and then made his way over to the warrior and led down beside him. All that day White Spirit never left the warrior's side. The young brave offered him water and food but White Spirit took nothing, he just sat by the warrior's side not moving. The young brave moved the warrior onto his side to change his dressing and see if the wound had improved but it was just the same. The warrior murmured something and then was silent. The young brave made him as comfortable as he could, wrapping him in his blanket and putting more wood on the fire. As night fell the young brave sat by the fire looking at the warrior and White Spirit hoping that he would regain consciousness. As he sat there he drifted in and out of sleep and this ritual went on for three days and nights and on the fourth night the young brave was awoken by White Spirit howling at the warrior's side. He stood up and went over to the warrior who was motionless and knelt down by his side. The young brave could see that he was not breathing and with tears running down his face he placed his hand over the warrior's face and closed his eyes. He stood up and yelled out "Why?" to the Great Spirits above, but there was silence. The young brave chanted all night and as daylight broke he knew what he had to do for his old friend to enable him to enter the Great Spirit World above. All that day the young brave collected wood and by nightfall he had built the wooden platform he needed. He returned to where the warrior was laying. He gently picked up the warrior's limp body and carried it up to the ledge where he gently placed him on the wooden platform, placing his hands together. He placed all the warrior's possessions around hi, and then covered him with his blanket. He stood back, tears flowing freely down his face, he did not want to say goodbye to his old friend but he knew he had to. At that moment he heard the cry of White Spirit and he knew it was time to let go of his dear friend. He knelt down and slowly lit the fire. It was not long before the complete wooden platform was engulfed in a red fireball burning brightly in the darkness. He just stood there, tears running down his face, he felt totally alone. As dawn started to break all that was left of the wooden platform he had built was a pile of ash, just smouldering. All that day he did not move, he just sat looking at the remains of the fire. A light wind blew through the canyon that afternoon and bit-by-bit the ledge was cleansed until there was nothing left. That night he sat by the fire thinking of his old friend, he felt sad and totally alone, the flames of the fire reflected in his face. At that moment he heard a voice saying, "Raise your eyes" and as he raised his head he could not believe what he saw. Stood right in front of him was the warrior and White Spirit. He said to the young brave, "Do not be sad for I am always with you. It was time for me to join the Great Spirits. You have all you need to be a great leader. The Indian people will follow you. Do not be afraid, trust what you feel inside, follow your own instincts. I have taught you everything I know the rest you will learn as you follow life's path". That night they talked about the past and the future. The warrior told the young brave, "When dawn breaks your journey will begin. Leave this place with an open heart but always remember we will always be with you, you only have to ask". As morning broke the young brave made his way down to where the two ponies had been grazing. It was no surprise to him to find there was only his pony grazing on the lush grass. He remembered the warrior saying to him that, "the pony is our means of getting to and from places". He smiled to himself knowing that they were all together. He mounted his pony and slowly rode out onto the vast grassy plain knowing the warrior was right, his journey was truly about to begin.

Chapter 4

The Beginning

As he slowly rode across the grassy plain he felt alone yet quite excited about what may lay ahead. The words his old friend had said to him kept going over and over in his head. That night he made camp at the bottom of a hilly ravine and as night fell he sat by the fire gazing into its deep firey glow. Occasionally he glanced up at the night sky, the stars twinkling brightly in the blanket of darkness. At that moment a shooting star glittered across the blackness. A tear ran down his face, he knew in his heart of hearts that this was a sign from his old friend high above looking down on him making sure that all was well. He placed more wood on the fire, led down on his blanket and drifted off to sleep. For some reason he slept soundly till morning when he was awoken by the sound of birds singing. The sun shone high in the sky and he could feel its warmth on his face. He reached for his water bag, took a drink and splashed some on his face. He looked around. His pony was grazing peacefully on the lush grass. His old friend was right – this was a truly beautiful place. He put out the fire and gathered his few possessions and walked over to his pony. Placing his bag and blanket on the pony's back he reached down for the reigns and they walked off across the vast plain. High above a single eagle hovered, just gliding on the wind currents, hardly moving his vast wings, soaring high in the deep blue sky above. He knew in his heart what he had to do, for once in his life he was not afraid of the challenges ahead for he knew deep down inside that what ever his destiny would uncover he would not have to face it alone for his old friend would always be with him to help and guide him in his hour of need. He and his pony walked for what seemed hours and eventually they stopped to drink from a small stream. He sat for a while taking in all the beauty around him. The green grass, the tall trees, birds singing, the sun shining bright, blue sky and white fluffy clouds that seemed to just float silently across the vast sky. This was nature at its best. No man on earth could spoil this. He looked at the crystal clear water bubbling and rippling over small rocks. He placed his hands into the water and splashed some over his face to remove some of the dust. It felt cold and sweet. He looked at his pony drinking from the stream and he smiled and said to his old friend "it's just you and me now. What ever happens we will always be together"? Without any hesitation his pony slowly walked over to him and pushed his arm with his head. Eagle Eyes looked at him and said "Running Wind we have to journey far but together we will conquer all challenges that are put in our path. I do not know what lies ahead but what I do know is we are not alone". At that moment Eagle Eyes was aware that they were not alone. He stood up and turned around. A short distance away were six braves on ponies staring at him, their faces covered with war paint. One came forward slowly and threw his spear which landed between Eagle Eyes' legs. Without thinking Eagle Eyes reached down picked up the spear and broke it into two pieces across his knee then threw it to the ground. He gazed at the brave who had thrown it for what seemed like eternity then to his amazement the brave cried out something and returned to the others and they all disappeared over the hill in a cloud of dust. Eagle Eyes stood there for a moment. He did not believe himself what he had just done but he had to believe it for the evidence was right in front of him, a cloud of dust disappearing over the hill, braves retreating from one man, truly a sight beyond belief. He felt happy, he felt strong, but he knew inside it was power and belief from the spirits above. He mounted Running Wind and they rode off in the direction of the fleeing braves. Truly this was the start of their journey.

It was not long before Eagle Eyes reached the top of the hill. He stopped and gazed down the valley. There were about thirty wigwams, women cooking, children playing, braves coming and going from their camp. He stood there taking it all in. He mounted Running Wind and slowly started down the valley towards the camp not knowing what sort of reception he would receive. He got to within twenty yards of the camp when everything became silent, women and children stood silently not moving an inch, even their dogs were silent. All eyes were on Eagle Eyes. The only sound to be heard was the hooves of Running Wind walking slowly towards them. At that moment a brave stepped forward and pulled an arrow and placed it on his bow and started to pull back the arrow. Eagle Eyes stopped, looked at the people and said, "Do not be afraid, I mean you no harm, I come in peace". The brave who had stepped forward released the arrow. The sound of the arrow being released made a swift windy sound. Within a split second Eagle Eyes' hand moved. As though in slow motion he grabbed the arrow before it entered his chest. The people stood there open mouthed, not believing what they had just witnessed. Eagle Eyes slid off Running Wind's back and slowly walked towards the brave who had fired the arrow. All the other people moved slowly back leaving just the brave and Eagle Eyes standing there. Eagle Eyes asked the brave "why did you fire your arrow? Is it because you are afraid? You have nothing to be afraid of, I am but one man". He handed the arrow back to the brave who said nothing; he just stood there motionless. Eagle Eyes said to him "come, introduce me to the rest of your people".

But there was only silence.

Night was approaching as Eagle Eyes warmed his hands by the fire. He asked, "Is there no one who will speak to me?" A small Indian girl walked towards him and Eagle Eyes held out his hand. An old Indian medicine man spoke out. "She is not frightened because she cannot see". Eagle Eyes stood up and walked over to the young girl and led her back to the fire and they both sat down. She was about eight years old with the most beautiful smile and peach like skin. Eagle Eyes stood up and said to the people "you should all be ashamed. It takes the courage of a child to break the silence between us". Eagle Eyes asked how long the child had been without sight. Once again the old medicine man spoke "she has never had sight, she was born blind". Eagle Eyes stood up. "Before this night is over this little girl's sight will be restored". The medicine man said, "That is impossible. She has been without sight for years. Only the Great Spirits above have the power of sight, they have done nothing before why should they do anything now?" Eagle Eyes looked at the old medicine man and said "I have been sent to unite the Indian people and to bring them together as one nation. To take them back to their old ways, away from killing and burning, back to peace and tranquillity, back to when we were a proud nation". The medicine man laughed, "You are one man, you have no powers. The arrow you caught was just luck!" Eagle Eyes said to the medicine man "I will prove to you all that I have been sent by the Great Spirits above". He knelt down beside the little girl and placed his hands on her eyes and began to chant. This went on for several hours and when he had finished he soaked a piece of cloth in some water and wrapped it around the young girl's eyes. He then said, "When the cloth is dry this little girl's eyesight will be restored". The medicine man laughed again. Eagle Eyes turned to him and said, "When morning breaks you will laugh at me no more". As daylight approached Eagle Eyes took off the cloth "open your eyes little one" he said. "What do you see?" "Blue sky" she replied. "Look down and tell me what colour moccasins I have on", "brown" she said. "Look over to the old medicine man and tell me what colour headdress he is wearing". "Black and white feathers" she said. Eagle Eyes turned to the people and said "the Spirits have spoken. You have seen it with your own eyes". The little girl's mother ran across and hugged the little girl and the little girl said, "Mummy I can see you. I do not have to rely on touch any more for now I can see all the beautiful things and beautiful colours you told me about". The people flocked around Eagle Eyes thanking him for what he had done for the little girl. Eagle Eyes spoke, "It is not me you should be thanking. You should all be raising your hands to the Great Spirit above for it is they who have created this miracle not me". That night they sat around a huge central fire eager to hear what Eagle Eyes had to say. He sat in silence just looking into their faces. He could feel the loss and see the hope in their eyes and even he felt a sense of belonging. As he sat there thoughts rushed though his mind; conversations he had had with his old friend. He could feel the warriors' presence. He raised his hands upwards and began to chant. Slowly one by one they followed Eagle Eyes' movements, all except the old medicine man who stood watching, chanting and shaking an old snake rattle. Eagle Eyes stood up and walked over to the old man and placed his hand on his shoulder. "Do not be afraid old man," he said. "I have not come here to take your place. I have been sent here to help you and show you all the way forward, to take you all on a journey of discovery to a land rich in every way you could think of. A land truly yours, a land truly at peace, a land full of natural beauty, a land that truly belongs to the Indian people". The old medicine man spoke "no land like this exists. This is just magic". "Silence" shouted Eagle Eyes, "you old man have lived far too long in the past, you must cast your vision to the future". Eagle Eyes turned to him and said, "If I can prove anything to you will you believe that I have been sent by the Great Spirits above?" The old man laughed, "What you say is impossible!" Eagle Eyes raised his hands and at that moment a blue mist descended and covered the camp. The Indian people seemed frightened so Eagle Eyes assured them no harm would come to them and they must remain quiet and still. He turned to the old medicine man and said, "I know the one person you would love to see is your son. The old man just laughed and said "My son is dead, he was killed in battle with the white man many moons ago". Eagle Eyes said to the old man "Look towards the centre of the light". The old man for once was silent for there in the middle of the light stood one figure that slowly started to walk forward towards the old man. Eagle Eyes looked at the old medicine man who looked frail and spoke to him softly, "Walk forward old man and greet your son, he has come a long way to see you". The old man seemed hesitant but finally he stepped forward and they both embraced one another. The blue mist seemed to engulf both figures, all around the air was silent yet a flute like sound could be heard faintly as if carried gently on the wind and the slow steady beat of a drum which seemed at times to get louder yet at other times seemed to return to its source. After a while the old medicine man emerged from the blue mist and walked slowly towards Eagle Eyes. He attempted to speak but no words were forthcoming. "Its alright" Eagle Eyes said "I can see the love in your eyes and the warmth in your heart".

Eagle Eyes told the old medicine man to rest. The blue mist still lingered but this time white stars seemed to focus on the centre, swirling around in a circular motion. Eagle Eyes was drawn to this white starlight circle and as he approached its centre he seemed to be drawn right into its light. Piercing light formed all around him and he shielded his eyes from the brightness. Then he heard a familiar voice calling to him to take away his hands and look straight ahead. Before him stood his old friend The Warrior and beside him sat White Spirit still as magnificent as ever. Stars twinkled all around them; their white colour seemed more intense than ever. "Hello Eagle Eyes" said The Warrior. He asked him how he felt about what he had seen and Eagle Eyes replied, "I asked the spirits for guidance and help and it is forthcoming but I still do not know if I am following their instructions". The Warrior walked towards him and placed his hand on Eagle Eyes' shoulder. It felt ice cold yet he could feel his friends' warmth throughout his body. The Warrior told him, "You have nothing to prove my friend, open your heart and go with your inner feelings. Tonight you have been guided by a Great Spirit force more powerful than you could imagine. Trust in your own ability, it is this alone that will put you and your people on the pathway of destiny". Eagle Eyes looked at his old friend with tears in his eyes and said, "I really miss you old friend. At times I feel the weight of leadership lays very heavy on my shoulders and yet at other times my heart leaps with joy when I am able to bring some kind of happiness into some person's life". The Warrior told Eagles Eyes, "Do not worry for you have only to ask for help and it will be given. I and White Spirit are always with you". As Eagle Eyes turned around to say something to his old friend he saw him and White Spirit disappear back into the white starlight which rose high in the sky then in a flash was gone. Eagle Eyes opened his mouth and said, "I wanted to ask you a question old friend" and in a split second The Warriors voice was carried on the wind, "the answer you seek is high above" he said. Eagle Eyes replied, "I do not understand" and The Warrior's reply was "seek the knowledge; this is where your answer is, look above". Eagle Eyes smiled. He remembered The Warrior showing him the mighty eagle soaring high in the sky. His question had been answered. At that moment the six braves returned. He remembered the brave who had thrown the spear at him and they both stood looking at one another. The brave asked the old medicine man what Eagle Eyes was doing in their village and the old man replied, "He has been sent by the great Spirits to lead us to the great lands of our ancestors". The young brave got very angry and started to walk towards Eagle Eyes, his hand on his knife. "Stop," said the old medicine man but the brave kept walking towards Eagle Eyes. As the brave raised his knife in the air Eagle Eyes placed his hand on the brave's shoulder and in a split second rendered him helpless on the ground. The brave could not move, he felt as if there was a heavy weight pinning him to the ground. Eagle Eyes knelt beside him and said, "Why are you filled with so much hatred, why are you so afraid of strangers"? He placed his hand on the brave's forehead and muttered something the brave did not understand, "since you were a child your head has been full of bad teachings. When I remove my hand all the hatred you feel will be gone and you can then start to live your life with more understanding and compassion for your fellow man". As the young brave rose to his feet he seemed to be in a daze, he just slowly walked over to the old medicine man and sat down. He said nothing he just kept looking at Eagle Eyes who was still kneeling on the ground.

Eagle Eyes raised his hands high above to give thanks to the Great Spirits. For once he felt he belonged. He felt an overwhelming need to lead his people to a better place, a place where they would not be persecuted anymore. A place where they could live their lives in harmony and peace.

The following day he gathered the people together and told them his thoughts and dreams. He told them of a land he had been shown by his old friend The Warrior. For once the people listened in silence, no one interrupted Eagle Eyes, they all sat listening to his every word. When he had finished he told them "in two moons I will be leaving this place to travel north to this land. Follow me and I will lead you to a land away from all starvation, a land where man does not kill man, a land where we can live in peace, a land where we will be shown the old ways of our forefathers". Eagle Eyes stood up and looked around at their faces. He looked deep into their eyes and said, "You all have the power inside to follow your heart". He told them to follow their dreams. He told them that they had been given a chance to regain their freedom – all they had to do was believe. The spirits above would protect them and show them the way forward. Eagle Eyes called out for Running Wind his trusted pony, which walked slowly over to him. Eagle Eyes climbed onto his back and slowly rode away. The old medicine man called out to him asking him where he was going and Eagle Eyes replied, "Do not worry old man, I will return in two moons and together we will all travel north. While I am gone think of all the things I have said to you" and in a split second Eagle Eyes was gone. All that remained was a cloud of dust.

Eagle Eyes rode on till dusk and stopped that night between a group of trees where a small stream of trickling water gently ran over small boulders. He made a fire and sat down to rest, the sound of the wind gently rustling the leaves had a truly calming effect on him. As he gazed into the fire his thoughts were taken back to the events and happenings that occurred with the Indian people. He gently drifted off to sleep only to be awoken by a piercing cry. For a moment he just lay there gathering his thoughts together and saying to himself, "did I hear this sound or did I dream it". It was not long before the piercing cry sounded again and again. Eagle Eyes jumped to his feet trying to identify from which direction it was coming. The piercing cry rang out again but this time it seemed to be carried on the wind. Eagle Eyes followed the sound for a short distance when he came across a very old tree with branches strewn around its massive base. It had come to the end of its life and was rotting away. He looked around but could see nothing but the branches from the old tree. Then he heard a rustling sound. As he walked closer the rustling sound got louder as if something was trying to break free. He hesitated for a moment trying to pinpoint exactly where this sound was coming from then he saw some movement just ahead of him. He slowly moved closer not wishing to frighten what ever was there. He bent down and moved a large branch and as he lifted it towards him he had the shock of his life for right in front of him was a beautiful eagle, its right wing trapped under the branches. He placed the branch on the ground and stood watching the magnificent bird with its white head and strong yellow beak, its eyes watching every move Eagle Eyes made as he stood wondering what to do next. It was then that he heard the gentle words of his old friend The Warrior, "Release him Eagle Eyes. Walk forward and lift the branch that traps his wing". Eagle Eyes looked around but his old friend was not there. He slowly walked over to the tree and lifted the branch. The eagle moved away from him slowly and stopped. Eagle Eyes sat down on the branch and watched as the eagle pruned his feathers. He had never been so close to an eagle before, he had only ever seen them soaring high in the sky. Then the magnificent bird opened his wings and moved them slowly back and forth, gaining pace with every movement. Eagle Eyes could feel the wind on his face with every movement the bird made with its wings. Suddenly the eagle gave out a loud cry and flew off circling the group of trees where Eagles Eyes had made camp. He stood up and made his way back to the fire and took a drink from his water bag. It was then he heard the mighty fluttering of wings and looked up. There sat on a high branch was the beautiful eagle. They both just looked at one another. Eagle Eyes took a piece of dry turkey meat in his hand and held it out towards the eagle. The bird looked and after a while flew down gently and landed about five feet away from Eagle Eyes who then knelt down and offered the meat to it. Slowly the bird walked over to him and took the meat gently from his hand then flew back up into the tree to eat it. Eagle Eyes returned to the fire. He felt happy as he wrapped his blanket around his shoulders and settled down for the night. It was not long before he drifted off to sleep but before dawn broke he was woken by a hand on his shoulder gently bringing him round. It was his old friend The Warrior. "What is wrong" Eagle Eyes asked, "nothing" replied the Warrior, "I have come to tell you that the eagle you helped tonight has been sent by the Great Spirits to guide you and the Indian people to the land of our freedom and peace. Watch his every move for he alone is the warrior of the sky. You will have to rely on his knowledge and skill for he alone carries all the hopes and dreams of the Indian nation". Eagle Eyes knew what his old friend The Warrior said was the truth, he could feel it deep down inside, an overwhelming feeling of inner peace. He had felt this feeling before but this time it was stronger. He turned to say something to his old friend but he had gone. Eagles Eyes smiled. He gazed up at the magnificent bird perched on a tall branch and said, "Well my friend, we have much to do". Daylight was starting to break, the darkness disappearing, slowly in the distance a deep blue sky was starting to make its presence. As he watched the sun broke high in the sky, its bright rays shining down warming the ground below. Eagle Eyes put out the remaining embers of the fire, collected his things and walked over to his pony placing his blanket over its back. He slid onto the pony's back and gently rode back towards the village. As he rode slowly over the wide-open plains he could hear the song of birds carried on the wind. He glanced up and there high in the sky circling was the magnificent eagle, its wings stretched fully out, hardly moving. He soared high in the sky and then, with little effort, dropped gently picking up the air currents. Eagle Eyes carried on and after about two hours riding he reached the top of a hill overlooking the village below. He stopped and gazed down. The village was just as he had left it. There had been nothing taken down and nobody was waiting, they were all going about their daily tasks. Eagle Eyes wondered why. He rode down to the village and as he approached he felt aware that things were not right. He stopped, slid off his pony's back and made his way over to where the old medicine man was sitting. He asked the old man why nobody had started to pack their belongings and he replied that they would not be going. Eagle Eyes stood up and asked the old man why. The old man replied, "Our young braves want to stay here and fight". Eagle Eyes shouted, "Have you people learned nothing? Killing solves nothing. I have been sent to show you all the way forward, the way to everlasting peace and harmony. If you stay here you will all die"! Eagle Eyes asked, "Where are all your young braves now". The old man replied, "They have gone hunting, they will be back by nightfall". Eagle Eyes replied, "Well old man I will wait and give you all one last chance to change your lives for ever. We will wait for your young braves to return and then you will all have your choice to follow me or your lives will be wasted for nothing. Your life's blood will seep slowly into the ground you all stand on". Eagle Eyes glanced round and looked deep into the eyes of all the people, they seemed to have a glazed look upon their faces. He sensed a feeling of despair and even a sense of loss. The air was silent and nothing was moving, everything was still. Then the silence was broken by a young woman's scream. Eagle Eyes glanced round in the direction of this tormented cry. He ran towards the wigwam that the cries were coming from. As he approached an old woman came out shouting. Eagle Eyes grabbed her with both arms and asked her what was the matter. She told him that the young girl inside was in childbirth but the baby was stuck and if the mother did not receive help quickly both of them would die. Eagle Eyes entered the wigwam and saw the young girl rolling around the floor in agony. He called to the old woman to fetch him clean cloth and plenty of hot water. By now all the people had gathered round the wigwam shouting for Eagle Eyes to come out and let the old medicine man go in. Eagle Eyes emerged with a stern look upon his face. He shouted at all the people who were gathered there, telling them that he was the only one who could save the life of the mother and child. He told them to be silent and listen, he told them to reach up and ask for forgiveness from the Great Spirits above for the lives of this mother and baby were in their hands. He then disappeared back into the wigwam to prepare himself for this most difficult task. He asked for guidance. He placed his hand on the young mother's forehead. She was sweating heavily. He kept telling her to trust him and he would relieve her pain. He placed a small piece of wood in her mouth and told her to bite on it hard for the pain would get worse before it got better. He told the old woman to keep bathing her forehead to try and keep her temperature down and he placed his hand on the young mother's stomach. He could feel that the baby's head was stuck. He inserted his hand slowly and he could feel the baby's head. He applied a rhythmic pressure downwards and sideways with his other hand. He gently tried to turn the baby's head very slowly. The baby's head turned. He called to the young mother to push one more time. She cried out in pain and in a split second the young baby's head emerged. Eagle Eyes noticed the cord around the baby's neck and quickly unwound it. He placed his mouth over the baby's mouth and blew as hard as he could. His first attempt failed. He tried again but this time he placed the young baby on a blanket and as he blew into its mouth he gently pressed down on the baby's chest. The baby let out a gasp and then started to cry. Eagle Eyes cut the cord, bathed the young baby and then wrapped him in the blanket. He told the old woman to take care of the young mother and emerged from the wigwam. He held the young baby high above his head in thanks for the Great Spirits guidance. He turned to the people who were dancing and laughing and told them to be silent. He told them this was a new life, a new beginning. He told them that in the morning he would be leaving. "Those of you who wish to follow me are welcome. Any of you who stay are foolish," he told them. "Yet again the Great Spirits have proved to you that they and they alone have the power of life and death, they have given you the choice, now the decision is yours. You can follow the path you are already on or you can follow your destiny, it is up to you". Eagle Eyes returned to the wigwam and placed the young baby to his mother's breast. The young baby started to feed. The young mother thanked Eagle Eyes for his help and Eagle Eyes replied, "Cherish your son for he in time will be a true leader of men. Now rest, you will need your strength for the journey ahead. When you are well again give thanks to the Great Spirits above for they alone have breathed life into your son for he has been chosen to carry on from me when my time comes to join the Great Spirits above". Eagle Eyes asked the young girl what her name was and she replied, "Running Stream". He also asked where her man was and she replied, "He is dead. I am alone". Eagle Eyes told her "you are not alone for I will look after you and from now on you will be known as Starlight". She started to say something and Eagle Eyes placed his fingers on her lips and said, "Rest". She closed her eyes and slept. As Eagle Eyes stood up he gazed down at the young baby fast asleep in his mother's arms. This was a sight he would never forget. At that moment the silence was broken by the sound of pony hooves thundering along the ground and the voices of high-spirited braves returning to the village. He heard voices and his name being called. Eagle Eyes emerged from the wigwam to be confronted by one young brave, angry that he had been involved in the birth of the young child. Eagle Eyes asked the brave why he was so angry. He replied that the young mother was the wife of his young brother who had been killed in battle with the white man many moons ago. Eagle Eyes felt this young brave's aggression and hatred towards him. He tried to calm him down but he could see the fire raging in the young brave's eyes. At that moment the young brave started to walk forward towards Eagle eyes, his knife already drawn from its sheath. Eagle Eyes stood his ground and told the young brave "I feel your hatred, I feel your fear, but you have nothing to be afraid of". At that moment a loud piercing cry from above could be heard. Everybody gazed upwards and high in the sky, circling, was an eagle, the light shimmering off his wing tips as he kept crying out, constantly circling the village below. The young brave shouted at Eagle Eyes, "It is just an eagle, it has no magical powers and neither do you, I will prove this to everyone here". Eagle Eyes still stood his ground and never moved. He told the young brave to stop but still he kept coming forward, the knife blade glinting in the fading light. Then without warning the piercing cry got louder and without any sound the magnificent bird drew in its wings and hurtled silently towards the ground. The young brave was unaware of what was about to happen within a few seconds. The eagle, its talons clenched, landed on the young brave's head. The people all moved back from the magnificent bird with its wings fully outstretched and calling out with its piercing cry. Eagle Eyes called out for it to release the young brave. After a few seconds the bird released its captive and flew off into a tall tree. The young brave by now was lying on the ground, blood pouring from his face. Eagle Eyes went across to where the young brave was lying. He was crying out in pain, his hands covered in blood. Eagle Eyes moved his hands and he could see that the young brave had lost one of his eyes. Eagle Eyes hit him, once only, to render him unconscious so he could inspect the injury properly. He took him inside the wigwam and bathed his face. One eye had been completely removed but the other was only slightly damaged, he covered both eyes, tomorrow morning would show whether he would be totally blind or if he still had some sight in the eye. All he could do now was wait. Outside the other braves grabbed their rifles and headed towards the big tree where the eagle had landed. Eagle Eyes shouted at them to stop. He asked them why they wanted to kill this magnificent bird. One of them said, "You have seen what this bird has done to our friend. He must die". Eagle Eyes stood in front of them and told them to put down their rifles. He told them that this was a time of peace and that the killings must stop. They walked past him. He again told them to "stop"; he told them that the eagle had been sent by the Great Spirits above. He told them that if one shot were fired against this bird the Great Spirits would avenge its aggressors. They stopped and returned to Eagle Eyes. He told them to go back and wait at the village, when he had news of their friend he would come and find them. Eagle Eyes returned to the wigwam. The young brave lay silently on the floor. Eagle Eyes replaced the cloth, which was soaked in blood, but before he covered the young brave's eyes he looked at the damage. Fortunately the remaining eye had very little damage to it; it was only the eye-lid that had been punctured. He was very lucky he had not lost both eyes. All that remained of the other eye was the socket. He looked at it carefully. It had stopped bleeding. Eagle Eyes sat with him all night. As morning dawned the young brave started to come round. Eagle Eyes explained to him that he had lost one eye and that he was lucky it was not both. The young brave got even more aggressive on hearing about his injury and vowed to seek revenge on the eagle. Eagle Eyes shouted at him in a stern voice "have you still not listened to the voice of the Great Spirits? What happened to you yesterday was a warning from above, if you do not listen now your life will end here, the choice is yours". Eagle Eyes went to find the young brave's friends. He told them that he was lucky, he had been given a second chance and that he still had the sight of one eye. He told them why he had been sent and that they were all welcome to follow him to a land of peace, but if they remained on the path of destruction they would all die. They looked at him but said nothing. He once again told them "this is a time for peace and harmony, the killings must stop. Those of you who do not follow me and choose to follow the path of violence will meet a bloody end. This I have seen through the Great Spirits eyes. Lay down your weapons of destruction and follow the path of peace". As Eagle Eyes started to walk away one of them shouted out "how do we know the words you speak are the truth"? Eagle Eyes replied, "You do not. The only way to find out is to follow me. You have nothing to lose but everything to gain. You are young and full of fight, put this to good use and make something of your lives". At that point the calmness was shattered by two shots ringing out. It was the young brave. He had left the wigwam with his rifle intent on killing the eagle that had taken his eye. Eagle Eyes shouted at him to stop but he carried on until his rifle was empty. He threw it to the ground in rage and started to climb the tree where the eagle was still perched. Eagle Eyes again told him to "stop and come down" but he still took no notice. He kept on climbing the tree until he was about five feet away from the eagle perched on a branch. As he got even closer to the eagle it let out a piercing cry but still the young brave carried on. The eagle flew upward. Its massive wings, fully out stretched, just brushed the top of the young brave's head but this was enough to put him off balance. He fell downwards smashing his head on the ground below. Eagle Eyes ran towards him. His young life ebbing away the young brave died at the foot of the big old tree. Eagle Eyes picked up the young brave in his arms. H e looked at the people and said, "We all have choices in this life and this young brave made his. It was the wrong choice. How many more of you have to die before you all realise that I am telling you the truth"? He took the lifeless body of the young brave to his friends. He asked them "is this what you want, for your lives to end like this? Your friend had a choice. He was given the chance, yet still he followed the path of hate and vengeance. It is a path of never ending torment and pain which in the end cost him his life and if you follow in his footsteps the same fate will await you. It is your life, do as you wish but never blame others for your own weakness". Eagle Eyes started to walk away. One of the young braves asked, "What should we do"? Eagle Eyes replied, "Follow your heart. Follow your inner feelings for it is they that will guide you and direct you on the right path". Eagle Eyes walked slowly up the rocky side of the hill overlooking the village. His heart felt heavy. Half way up he reached a large protruding piece of rock pushing straight out from the hillside. He sat there, his head cupped in his hands. He wondered if there was anything he could have done to change what had happened to the young brave. At that moment he felt a presence. A warmth seemed to surround him yet it was starting to get dark and the sun was going down. It was then he felt a hand on his right shoulder, but when he turned his head there was no one there but the pressure from the hand remained. Eagle Eyes smiled yet at the same time tears ran down his face for he knew deep inside that it was his old friend the Warrior coming to him in his hour of need. He asked the Warrior if he had done the right thing with the young brave. The Warrior replied "Eagle Eyes you could have done nothing more. He chose his path and only death awaited him. You have travelled a very long way in a short time, a lot has been laden on your shoulders but not once have you buckled under this heavy pressure". He told Eagle Eyes, "Look down at the people below. They are getting ready to leave. It is your word and your insight that gives them the courage and belief to follow you to the peaceful haven you have promised. Go forth my friend. Never doubt your capabilities for I will always be there to guide you in your hour of need. Now go to your people for it is you they need now". Eagle Eyes stood up and gazed around but there was nothing there except the outline of a handprint on his right shoulder. Eagle Eyes just smiled to himself for he knew that that alone was a sign from his old friend The Warrior. He made his way back down to the village where the people were busy taking down their tepees and packing away their belongings in readiness for the journey ahead. Eagle Eyes at last felt a sense of belonging. He gazed around at the people all busy packing away their possessions, now they were all working together, young helping old, adults helping children, everyone working together in perfect harmony. "At last" he thought, "we are all starting to achieve something truly beautiful". Could this be the start? He hoped in his heart of hearts that this was the day the Indian nation started to listen and to learn. Only time would tell for there was still much more to do. He walked across to Starlight who was holding her son and helped her to gather her belongings together. He then walked over to his pony, reached down for the reigns and led him over to where Starlight was standing. He placed her on his pony's back and then gave her son to her to hold in her arms. She told Eagle Eyes that she could walk like the rest of the people but Eagle Eyes told her she must look after herself and save her strength for she had her son to think of now. Eagle Eyes placed the few possessions

Starlight had over his shoulder and picked up the reigns of his pony and gazed around. Everyone was waiting. He slowly started to walk away glancing back now and then. It was a truly magnificent sight to see all the people following. Those who had difficulty walking were being helped by those stronger and able to carry them. It brought a tear to Eagle Eyes who gazed up above to give thanks for what was now taking place. It had taken a long time but now the people were truly working together. Eagle Eyes gazed up at the deep blue sky with its white fluffy clouds that seemed to drift endlessly across the vast blue open space. High above, circling around them, was the magnificent eagle showing them the way ahead. A light wind blew across the plains, the long grass bowing to its gentle breeze. After a few hours Eagle Eyes stopped so they could rest a while. He lifted Starlight off Running Wind's back and they sat together on the grass talking. Eagle Eyes passed her his water bag. She took a drink from it then poured some into her hand and rubbed it over her young son's face. He started to cry, "He is hungry", she said. She placed her son to her breast and he started to feed. Eagle Eyes smiled. All was well. The old medicine man came forward and asked Eagle Eyes how long it would take to reach the land of peace. Eagle Eyes replied, "Four moons at the pace we are travelling now". Eagle Eyes told the people "we may as well stop here tonight then we can all start fresh in the morning". He looked around at the people. They looked tired as they started to gather wood and small fires started to appear around them. Eagle Eyes gathered some wood to make a fire. In a few hours it would be dark. As darkness fell he could hear the chatter and laughter of his people settling down for the night. It felt good, it felt heart warming, it felt right. His people had endured a great deal of misery and pain and it was good to see them finally looking happy. Starlight wrapped her son in a blanket and rocked him to sleep in her arms. It was not long before he was sound asleep. She placed him down by her side and handed Eagle Eyes some food. Eagle Eyes thanked her for the food when he had finished and they sat by the fire talking. Starlight asked Eagle Eyes how it had all started and Eagle Eyes told her of his childhood. He also told her what happened to his parents and how his life had changed when he met the Warrior. He told her how he was shown the old ways, how the Great Spirits and the Warrior had turned his life around and now it was his turn to show the Indian people that through peace they will be rewarded by being given the promised land. Starlight hung on his every word. He looked up at the night sky "Look" he said to her, "right there, a shooting star". She gazed in amazement as she told him "I have never seen anything so bright". Eagle Eyes told her to get some rest as he wanted to make an early start in the morning. Starlight placed her son between them; their body heat would keep her son warm through the night. That night they all slept well. The following morning dawned and they were awakened by the sound of birds singing and the sun showering them with its heat. It was going to be another beautiful day. Eagle Eyes splashed some water over his face; Starlight took a drink and then fed her son who was crying. Eagle Eyes packed everything away in readiness for the journey ahead. He glanced around. The people had packed away their belongings and were ready to leave. Eagle Eyes lifted Starlight onto his pony's back then handed her son to her to hold in her arms. Eagle Eyes took hold of Running Wind's reigns and they slowly moved off together. They had been walking for about three hours when their harmony was broken by a screech from above. Eagle Eyes stopped and looked upwards. He could see the eagle circling in the distance. The old medicine man asked Eagle Eyes what was wrong and he replied, "The eagle has sent me a warning". He lifted Starlight down off his pony's back and told them all to wait there while he went to see what the eagle was warning them of. He mounted Running Wind and rode of in the direction of the eagle. He had been riding for about thirty minutes when he came to the place the eagle was circling. He got off Running Winds back and looked around. There in the distance he could see soldiers riding. He mounted his pony and returned to where his people were waiting. The old medicine man asked Eagle Eyes what was the matter and he replied, "Soldiers are heading this way but do not worry, if you do what I say they will not see you and ride straight by". Eagle Eyes gathered all the people behind him. The people were silent and still and Eagle Eyes raised his hands upwards and said "Great Spirits protect us, send me a dust storm to separate my people from the soldiers". Within seconds the wind started to gain pace and tumbleweeds were blow through the air. Eagle Eyes told his people to cover their eyes and mouths, as the wind would get worse. The dust cloud seemed to form a moving wall. They could see nothing but dirt and weeds being blown at a terrific pace in front of them. Eagle Eyes knew that if this was the only thing he could see then the dust cloud would be the only thing the soldiers could see. After a while they could hear the horses and gun carriages passing in front of them yet they could still only see the dust cloud. After about an hour all they could hear was the wind blowing in all its fury. Eagle Eyes raised his hands in thanks to the Great Spirits and as he lowered them the wind dropped to virtually nothing. As the dust cloud cleared all that could be seen was the grass gently moving in the breeze. There was no trace of any soldiers. The people looked at Eagle

Eyes in amazement. He just smiled and said "Let us carry on, we still have a few hours of daylight left". As they followed Eagle Eyes he could hear them chatting amongst themselves about the past event. Eagle Eyes told them to be silent and save their energy for the journey. They looked at him baffled, even Starlight looked at him but she said nothing. They all carried on in silence. That night as they made camp Starlight asked Eagle Eyes why he had told the people to be silent. He replied, "What happened was for a reason. The Great Spirits helped us in our hour of need. I do not want the people to think that this will always happen when they are in trouble because it will not. They must never take things for granted for disappointment will always follow. Always have trust and belief in the spirits above for they will never let you down unlike man who will promise you everything but give you nothing". Eagle Eyes told the old medicine man to tell the people this.

Eagle Eyes sat down with Starlight that night but no words were spoken. It was as if Eagle Eyes was not with her, he was there in body but his spirit was elsewhere. She sat looking at him wondering when he would speak when suddenly the silence was broken by wolves howling in the distance. Eagle Eyes still said nothing but stood up and walked slowly off into the darkness. It was as though he was being drawn into the blackness of the night. After a short time a bright light appeared in front of him. He shielded his eyes from its brightness then he heard a voice. He knew well it was his old friend The Warrior. The voice told Eagle Eyes to take his hands away from his eyes and as he did so, there, stood right in front of him, were his old friends The Warrior and White Spirit. The Warrior asked him why he had told his people to be silent when it was he who had asked for help from the Great Spirits. Eagle

Eyes told the Warrior that the people were taking these miracles for granted, they were thinking that the Spirits would stop any tragedies from happening. The Warrior told Eagle Eyes to "Stop!" He told him, "these are simple people, they believe what they see and hear. You have been privileged to have seen the Great Spirits, you have seen what they achieve, they have not. Be patient with them, they have a lot to learn, try to be a bit more understanding with them. You have nearly completed your task, we are all very proud of you. Now return to your people and remember what I have said to you". Eagle Eyes returned to Starlight who was sat by the fire. He told her he was sorry and she asked him if everything was all right. He said that it was and placed his arm around her shoulder. He told her their journey would be ending shortly and that the land he spoke of was only a day's ride ahead. Everyone settled down for the night and the following morning they were all up early and ready for the final part of their journey. Everyone was in good spirits. As the day progressed Eagle Eyes looked upwards. The eagle was circling high above a tall canyon a short distance ahead. As they got closer Eagle Eyes told the people they must stay here until daybreak the next morning. The medicine man asked Eagle Eyes, "Why can't we travel a little further? We still have hours of daylight left". Eagle Eyes told the old man "This is the place we will be given a sign". The old man replied, "All I see is high rock either side. There is no land here"! Eagle Eyes told him, "When daylight breaks a beam of light will hit that tall peak of rock over there" and pointed into the canyon, "then it will beam down showing us the opening", then he told the old man to go and tell the people what he had said. Eagle Eyes sat down with Starlight and her son as a light breeze blew across the plain's grass. He told Starlight, "When dawn breaks we will be shown the doorway to everlasting peace and harmony". As night began to fall there was laughter in the camp, the flames of the fires reflecting in the people's faces. The sky was lit with beautiful white twinkling stars and Starlight and Eagle Eyes gazed up at them as they drifted off to sleep.

As dawn began to break everyone was ready to move. As the sun rose higher over the tall peaks of rock a bolt of light hit the other side of the canyon wall showing them an opening at the bottom. They all made their way into the canyon and as they approached the opening they could see they would only be able to go through it one at a time. The entrance was dark and as Eagle Eyes asked the Great Spirits for light the inside was filled by a beautiful blue light, which reflected off the rock surface. One by one they entered and kept moving forward. After about an hour they emerged onto a beautiful wide-open green plain where deer were grazing on the lush grass. The people gazed in silence. Eagle Eyes gathered them together and told them that this was the place where they could live in peace and harmony. He told them to erect their tepees and let their ponies graze. Eagle Eyes erected Starlight's tepee near a small brook that ran from the rocks. She had made a fire and was preparing a meal for them when she suddenly looked up at him and knew he would not be staying long with her. When she asked him he replied, "I will be leaving when everyone is settled, leaving to find more Indian people and bring them to this place, but" he told her, "for now enjoy what you have for when I return it will be for good. This is the place where I can feel my forefathers. Their spirits roam free here. At last the Indian people are home".

Chapter 5

The Gatherer

Many moons had passed since Eagle Eyes had brought his people to this land of harmony and peace. As each day passed the feeling she had inside grew stronger, he knew in his heart the day was drawing closer when he would have to leave this beautiful place and search for more of his troubled people. Since he had brought his people to this harmonious land he could see the contentment and fulfilment on their faces. No more was there starvation, no more was there hatred, his people were learning to enjoy life. For once they were free. They had learnt the old ways again, hunting with bows and arrows and only killing what was necessary for them to live. Nothing was wasted; animal pelts were made into clothing and moccasins. Children ran around the village playing, women washed the clothes and cooked meals on the fires, it was good to see. Eagle Eyes felt he had achieved something.

Starlight looked at Eagle Eyes, no words were spoken yet she knew and that night as they sat by the fire she asked Eagle Eyes when he was going. He placed his arm around her and told her she had a very wise head on her shoulders. She smiled. He told her he would be leaving in two moons and as he looked into her eyes a tear ran down her cheek. He held her closer and kissed her on the cheek. "Do not worry, for when I return I will never leave you or your son again. In the short time we have been together I have grown to love you more and more each day. I will teach your son the values he needs to know for it is he who will lead the people when it is my turn to join the great spirits". She held Eagle Eyes' hand tightly. "But do not worry, that will not be for a long time yet". She told him, "I know you have to go but I worry you will not return". Eagle Eyes looked deep into her eyes and told her "you have nothing to worry about, the Great Spirits will not let any harm come to me". For the rest of the night they held each other tight, the flames flickering in their faces.

Dawn started to break through the darkness, another new day was about to start. As the sun started to show its brightness people started to emerge from their tepees. Women started to gather wood for their fires. It was not long before the sound of laughter could be heard from children running around the tepees. Eagle Eyes looked up towards the Great Spirits and gave thanks. Starlight handed Eagle Eyes some water to drink and as they gazed at each other Eagle Eyes noticed tears running silently down her face. He stood up and drew her close to him and placed his hands gently on her face, his thumbs gently wiping the tears away, but with each movement of his hands the tears were replaced time and time again. He held her even tighter and kissed her face gently. They both stood there silently, no words were spoken. After a while he whispered gently in her ear "I love you". She held him even tighter. By now people had started to gather around them but nobody said a word. At that moment the old medicine man placed his hand on Eagle Eyes' shoulder and asked him what was wrong. Eagles Eyes turned his head and looked straight into the old man's eyes and told him that Starlight was upset. The old man said to Eagle Eyes, "You do not have to go! You have brought us to this beautiful, peaceful place, stay with us". Eagle Eyes replied, "Even one as old as you with all the things you have seen in your lifetime must understand my quest is not completed, for in one moons' time I must leave this beautiful place and search for my people. You all are now safe and free to live out your lives in peace without fear of anyone or anything, my people are still out there suffering. They deserve the same chances that you all have been given". At that moment Starlight, still sobbing, ran towards her tepee and disappeared inside. The old medicine man bowed his head and gently placed his hands on Eagle Eyes' shoulder and told him, "Starlight has a broken heart, she knows you have to go but she is frightened you will not return. Go to her, she needs your reassurance and love. Talk to her until she understands". Eagle Eyes looked at the old man and he could see the wisdom in his eyes and he knew what he had to do. He said nothing but walked over to Starlight's tepee, pulled down the flap and disappeared inside. Eagle Eyes looked at Starlight who was sat with her young son sobbing in the corner of the tepee. He spoke to her softly placing his arm around her shoulders. He told her how much he loved them both and how heart broken he was that he had to leave. Starlight started to say something to Eagle Eyes but he placed his fingers on her lips. She gazed at him, tears running down her face. Eagle Eyes held them both tightly and told her she had his promise that he would return to her and her son forever when his quest was completed. The three of them sat for hours holding on to one another tightly as if their very existence depended on it. Suddenly a blue light appeared inside the tepee. Starlight grasped Eagle Eyes even tighter. Eagle Eyes smiled. "Do not be frightened Starlight, for what you are about to see is a sign from the Great Spirits". Eagle Eyes turned round to face the centre of the blue light and within seconds a figure and a wolf moved slowly towards them. Eagle Eyes stood up to greet his old friend the Warrior and White Spirit. The Warrior told Eagle Eyes to sit. He also spoke softly to Starlight and told her not to be afraid. "I have been sent by the Great Spirits above to help and reassure you. Eagle Eyes has much work to do and many moons of travelling before his quest is over and he can return to you". Starlight gazed in amazement at the figure in front of her, both he and the wolf were surrounded by the blue light. The Warrior held out his hand and asked Starlight to place her hand in his. As she slowly placed her hand in his she felt an overwhelming heat. The Warrior told her, "Do not worry for this feeling will soon pass". He told her to close her eyes and tell him what she could see. She told the Warrior, "I can see hundreds of people being killed for nothing. I can see children crying over their dead mothers. I can see starvation and disease, bodies laying everywhere". She let go of the Warriors hand and opened her eyes. She asked the Warrior "Why are you showing me these things?" and he replied "These things are real. They are happening now. People are dying even as we speak. This is why Eagle Eyes has to go and save as many people as he can. The people here are all safe, all the others are not. They have only one chance. Eagle Eyes must find as many as he can and bring them back to this place before the Indian nation as we know it is wiped off this earth for ever". Starlight was silent. The Warrior stood up and White Spirit looked up at him. "I know" he said and placed his hand on White Spirit's head. He looked at Eagle Eyes and said, "Remember, we will both be with you". He then told Starlight "You have nothing to fear, Eagle Eyes will return to you and your son". At that moment the Warrior and White Spirit disappeared into the centre of the blue light and within seconds the blue mist was gone. All that remained inside the tepee was Eagle Eyes, Starlight and her son. She held onto Eagle Eyes hand tightly and looked at him and said, "Now I understand why you have to go and I know deep in my heart that you will return". Eagle Eyes said nothing, he just held her tightly for he knew that in a few hours he would have to leave this beautiful place and the two people he loved so much for the rest of his people. His life could not carry on till his quest had been completed.

As dawn started to break Eagle Eyes gently laid Starlight down and covered her with his blanket. He gently kissed her and her son on their foreheads and slowly made his way to the entrance of the tepee without making a sound. He glanced quickly at the both of them – he did not want to leave but deep down inside he knew he had to. He slowly lifted the flap and made his way outside lowering the flap quietly behind him. There outside waiting for him was his trusted pony and the old medicine man. The old man thanked Eagle Eyes for everything he had done for his people. Eagle Eyes replied, "There are no thanks necessary. This was the will of the Great Spirits". Eagle Eyes asked the old man to look out for Starlight and her son until he returned. This he said he would do. They shook hands and in the blink of an eye Eagle Eyes was gone. As he made his way through the narrow passage his thoughts were with Starlight and her son who he had left behind. At that moment he heard the voice of his old friend The Warrior who said to him, "Look forward Eagle Eyes for they will be waiting for you when you return". Eagle Eyes pony gained speed, running through the narrow passageway of the mountain. It was as if they were being carried by the wind for as Eagle Eyes glanced down he could see that his pony's hooves were not touching the ground yet behind them there was a cloud of dust following them. After about an hour they reached the opening leading out onto the plain between the two peaks. Eagle Eyes knew this was the beginning of his quest. He rode on till the light started to fade and that night, as he sat by the fire his thoughts were of his people. He knew deep inside the misery they were suffering. He placed his blanket around his shoulders and tried to sleep but his thoughts of Starlight were still fresh in his mind. Eventually he dropped off to sleep but was awakened by the cries of wolves in the distance. He knew it was time for him to go and find his people. He mounted Running Wind and rode off across the plain. It was still dark but he knew that within two hours the sun would be rising. Mixed thoughts ran through his mind, even he did not know what lay ahead. As the darkness started to fade Eagle Eyes stopped and gazed upwards. The sun's rays were just starting to break through and Eagle Eyes could feel its warmth on his face. He closed his eyes for a moment. It was shortly after he heard the piercing cry of an eagle. He opened his eyes and gazed upwards and straight away he recognised the wise old bird circling high above him. He raised both hands as a gesture of thanks to the Great Spirits. He carried on riding for a couple of hours then stopped to rest and as he sat a strange sensation swept through his body. It was as if he was being carried somewhere else and yet he was aware that his body was firmly seated on the ground. As he took a drink from his water bag he was interrupted by the cries of the eagle above, the magnificent bird gliding higher and lower on the wind's currents. Even Eagle Eyes' pony, Running Wind, was restless. Something was wrong. Eagle Eyes knew deep inside that he had to move, and move fast, for something was driving them all onward, an overwhelming feeling to move quickly. Eagle Eyes mounted Running Wind who carried him swiftly across the grassy plain. It was not long before he heard the sound of gunfire in the distance and he could see smoke rising high in the sky. His friend the eagle was flying frantically above, circling the same spot time and time again. Running Wind moved swiftly across the ground, his hooves hardly making contact, it was as if they were being carried through the air. As Eagle Eyes reached the place where the eagle had been circling he could not believe the sight that met his eyes. His people were being cut to pieces by cavalry soldiers. The bodies of women and children were strewn around the village. Eagle Eyes cried out with rage. He raised both hands to the Spirits above and asked for guidance. The sky turned black, lightening flashed across the darkness and Eagle Eyes felt the power from above enter his body as he raced down towards the village. All he could think of was his people suffering at the hands of the soldiers. He suddenly felt something in his hands, it was a lance, but this was no ordinary lance for this one breathed fire. As he got closer to the village soldiers began to shoot at him. He yelled out and directed the fire from the lance at them and they fell from their horses. He carried on riding until all the soldiers were dead. Eventually Running Wind stopped and Eagle Eyes slipped from his back and just stood there wondering why. What was the reason? What was to gain from the death of his people? All these questions yet no answers! He stopped and knelt by the body of a young woman who had been virtually cut in two by a soldier's sword. As he gently turned her over he noticed a tiny hand covered by a shawl. As he gently unwrapped it a young baby girl emerged and he picked her up. Apart from her mother's blood on her she was not harmed. She was very lucky her mother had protected her even though she had lost her own life. Eagle Eyes wrapped her up and placed her in a cloth pouch. He then began looking around to see if anyone else was alive, he spent hours just looking around, the bodies lying where they fell. To him this had been senseless, what possible fight could these people have put up, most of the bodies were women and children apart from a few old men! No young braves were here. He laid the bodies side by side. There were thirty two - twenty women, five old men and seven children. Eagle Eyes wept as he laid down the last child's body. The smell of death lay heavy on the air. Everything was quiet, no birds singing, now wind blowing, just silence. Eagle Eyes raised his hands to the sky and shouted, "Why did you allow this to happen? You sent me here to save these people and yet you let me arrive too late. What good am I to these poor people?" At that moment Eagle Eyes felt a hand on his shoulder and with tears rolling down his cheeks he slowly turned around to be greeted by his old friend The Warrior, who told him "All things happen for a reason" and Eagle Eyes replied "I have never questioned you before but I cannot understand why the Great Spirits let this slaughter happen. It was senseless and unnecessary. These people had done nothing. They did not deserve to die. Thirty two bodies lay here, only one baby girl lives". The Warrior told Eagle Eyes "Always from death comes life, these people have passed to a better place, it was their time to go. Always remember it is better to have saved one life than none at all". He told Eagle Eyes "You have seen many tragedies, many lives wasted and before your quest is over you will see many more, but always remember life is for living, you could not help these people but there are many more you can help". The Warrior looked at the bodies laid side by side and raised his hands from his sides. White lightening flashed and within an instant, one by one the bodies were lifted gently onto a long wooden platform that had appeared in the sky. As the last child's body was laid to rest The Warrior asked Eagle Eyes to stand and told him to do as he did. Together they chanted and raised their hands upwards to the Great Spirits. Blue and white lights flashed across the sky. Eagle Eyes could see the outlines of braves riding ponies, their hooves pounding the night sky. Flames could be seen coming from the brave's lances as they headed towards the wooden platform. Below, Eagle Eyes shielded his eyes from the intense light but The Warrior told him "Look. These braves have been sent by the Great Spirits above to claim these people". Suddenly a blue and white light completely engulfed the platform and within seconds a tunnel of light shot upwards ending in a bright flash of white stars that disappeared into the blackness. The Warrior told Eagle Eyes "It is now over for these people, they are home. You must continue your search." At that moment the silence was broken by a baby's cry. Eagle Eyes turned around and picked up the young girl and cuddled her in his arms. The Warrior smiled, "I expect she is hungry, here give her this". He handed Eagle Eyes a small pouch containing milk, "you will find she will sleep till daylight". Eagle Eyes turned around to say something to The Warrior but he was gone. He sat there cuddling the child till daybreak pondering his thoughts of the nights' events. As the sun started to break through the darkness Eagle Eyes could feel its golden rays upon his face. He laid the child gently down on his blanket, she was sound asleep and did not stir. He started to gather his things together and as he looked around the village all that remained there was the charred bodies of the soldiers and their horses lying still in the dust. Eagle Eyes felt nothing for these soldiers deserved to die for the terrible pain and suffering they had inflicted on his people. As he walked across to his faithful pony Running Wind, he noticed a small basket lying on the ground. He picked it up and walked across to where the young child was sleeping. He laid a blanket inside and gently lifted the child into it. At least, he thought, it would make her more comfortable and it would shade her from the sun's heat. He laid the basket on Running Wind's back and secured it gently with some cowhide strips. He picked up the pony's reins and slowly walked off, away from this place of carnage. High above the eagle circled the place of death and then without any warning he let out one piercing cry, as if he was saying goodbye to the souls of the people who had died there. Eagle Eyes gazed up at the magnificent bird as he flew higher and higher deep into the blue sky, his large wings hardly moving on the winds currents. Eagle Eyes glanced at the child who was fast asleep. Eagle Eyes felt so sad. This young child had not yet started to live yet she had already lost her mother at a time when she really needed her. For the time being all he could do was look after her and give her all his love and affection and hope this would be enough until he could find a substitute mother for her.

Days came and went and they travelled over vast amounts of land, always in search of his people but finding nothing.

One day, as Eagle Eyes prepared the child for another day's journey he was aware that something was different. As he placed the child's basket on the pony's back he knew he was not alone. He gazed upwards and there on the hill sat about forty braves just watching him. He could see the dust cloud behind them - they had not been there long. Eagle Eyes returned to where the child was laying, picked her up and sat down. The braves just sat on their ponies looking at him. After about an hour they started moving slowly down the hill towards him. As they got closer Eagle Eyes could see these were renegade braves, their faces painted with black, white and red stripes. All they were searching for was a fight. Eagle Eyes placed the child on the blanket and stood in front of her. The braves stopped and one of them slid from his pony and slowly walked towards Eagle Eyes who stood silently waiting for the brave to say something. As he got closer Eagle Eyes could see the hate in his eyes. He stopped and told Eagle Eyes that they had been tracking him for days and he wanted to know where all his people were. He told Eagle Eyes that the young child was his daughter. As they sat Eagle Eyes told him what had happened, how the soldiers had killed all his people. The young brave stood up, he was angry, he wanted to know "where are all the bodies of my people"? Eagle Eyes told him that the Great Spirits had taken them. The young brave looked at Eagle Eyes with eyes piercing with hatred. As he moved forward towards him Eagle Eyes asked him "have you not had enough of killing? Does this land have to run red with blood before you stop"? The young brave's hand slid towards his knife. Eagle Eyes in a flash placed his hand on the young braves shoulder and told him, "I do not want to hurt you". As the young brave struggled to release his knife, Eagle Eyes gripped his arm firmly. The young brave called out to the others for help and as they got closer Eagle Eyes raised his other arm and directed them to stop. No matter how hard they tried they could not move any further. They could see and hear everything but they could not move. The young brave was silent. He could not understand how one man had all this power. Eagle Eyes asked the young brave to listen. He told him he had been sent by the Great Spirits to lead the Indian people away to a peaceful place, a land where they could live in peace, a land without fear. Eagle Eyes told him "I can show you this place or you can die, the choice is up to you". Eagle Eyes released his hold on the brave who stood for a moment before returning to the others. He jumped onto the back of his pony and sat there for a moment looking at Eagle Eyes, no words were spoken and then without any warning they were gone, all that remained was dust floating silently in the air. Eagle Eyes returned to the child who thankfully was still sleeping. As he gazed at her peaceful face he knew that this child and many more like her were the future of the Indian nation. Unfortunately, attitudes like her father's remain in the past. As he sat pondering his thoughts he could feel a presence, yet he could see nothing. He knew deep in his heart that his old friend The Warrior was with him. As Eagle Eyes prepared the child's milk he glanced down at her face and she smiled at him. Her beautiful deep black eyes were piercing yet he could see and feel the love that this child so young was giving. He gently cradled her in his arms and placed the small milk pouch to her mouth and she began to feed. This was a sight that Eagle Eyes would never forget. When she had finished he gently laid her on the blanket. He poured some water into a small bowl and gently began to bathe the child. She was smiling and chuckling and Eagle Eyes smiled back. He wrapped her in the blanket and rocked her to sleep in his arms. When she was asleep he gently laid her down. He collected some wood and started a fire - this would keep her warm through the night. As darkness fell Eagle Eyes sat by the fire. The only sound was the wood crackling, the embers glowing in the darkness. Now and again he could hear wolves cry's in the distance. He glanced at her, the reflection of the fire dancing across her face. He knew this was one of the most beautiful visions he would ever see. He gazed up at the night sky. Stars were shining in the blackness, it was as if they were floating, motionless yet their presence could be felt. At that moment a shooting star flashed across the darkness, disappearing into the distance. Eagle Eyes knew this calmness would be short lived for he could feel something. A worrying feeling crept over him. As he gazed at the child he knew that what ever happened she must live and many more like her. It was the only way for the Indian nation to survive. Too many of his people had died already.

The black sky started to lighten as dawn approached and Eagle Eyes gathered his things together. He moved silently, not wishing to wake the child. He gently lifted her and placed her on his pony's back. He then slowly and quietly placed handfuls of dirt on the fire putting out the last remaining embers that were still glowing. By now the sun was starting to rise and Eagle Eyes could feel its warmth as he grasped his pony's reins and move slowly forward. After a few hours Eagle Eyes stopped. The child was crying and he gently placed the small bag containing milk to her lips and she began to feed. As he took a drink from his water bag the silence was shattered by gunfire in the distance. Eagle Eyes moved quickly yet silently towards the sound he knew could mean only one thing. What lay ahead was not good. As he approached all he could see were a few ponies standing together, bodies of braves lay strewn around motionless. Tears ran down his face. He knew that these braves were the same ones who were with the child's father. He looked at them. All were dead apart from two who were only slightly wounded. As he turned them over one of them was only a boy. Luckily he had only been grazed on the left side of his head. Eagle Eyes gently lifted his head and bathed the wound. The boy muttered something but Eagle Eyes could not understand and then he was silent. Eagle Eyes knew that with rest he would recover. As he turned the last brave over he realised it was the child's father. Luckily he too was only slightly wounded. Eagle Eyes bathed his wound and made him as comfortable as he could. Eagle Eyes knew he had to survive, not only for the child's sake but also to answer for the many lives that he had destroyed. It took many hours but finally both started to regain consciousness. The child's father was the first to come round. He sat up, opened his eyes and looked around. He said nothing. Eagle Eyes spoke to him and told him that he was responsible for the deaths of all the braves that lay there motionless. The brave stood up and Eagle Eyes could see the hatred in his eyes. Eagle Eyes said to him "surely your hatred has been satisfied! How many more of my people have to die through your ignorance"? Finally the brave spoke and he told Eagle Eyes, "These braves that lay here are warriors and have earned their place with the Great Spirits". Eagle Eyes replied "Yes they will be with the Great Spirits but because they followed you they have joined them before their time". The brave looked at Eagle Eyes but said nothing. Eagle Eyes knew that unless he could convince him, this brave's path would end in certain death. Night fell and as they sat by the fire the only sounds to be heard were the embers crackling, its red glow flickering on their faces. Eagle Eyes checked on the child – she was sleeping soundly. He wrapped his blanket around her tightly to protect her from the cold night air and returned to the fire. The brave and the young boy were talking but as Eagle Eyes approached they were silent. Eagle Eyes asked them why the silence. The brave looked at Eagle Eyes and said "The warriors that followed me died with honour. I am sorry that I was not with them when they joined the Great Spirits". Eagle Eyes looked at the young boy and asked "Is this what you feel?" The young boy just looked at Eagle Eyes and said nothing. After a short silence Eagle Eyes told both of them "What happened here was pointless, a complete waste of life. Your braves were killed because your enemy was stronger. You had the choice to save them yet you led them to their deaths. You and this young boy were saved by the Great Spirits so that you can learn from your mistakes. You both have one chance only. You and only you have the choice to live or to die. You both should reflect on those braves who died here and the price they paid to satisfy your hatred". Eagle Eyes said to the brave "give me your hand, I want to show you something". Eagle Eyes waited with his hand held out and eventually the brave placed his hand firmly in Eagle Eyes grasp. After a short while voices could be heard calling out. The brave tried to pull his hand away but it was held firmly in Eagle Eyes grip. The voices got louder. They kept telling the brave that the path he was travelling would end in certain death unless he changed his ways. At that moment the voices stopped and there in front of them was a thick blue mist with a bright white light surrounding it and then spirit brave after spirit brave emerged from the mist, each figure surrounded by the bright white light. They all gathered in front of them and the brave tried to pull away. Eagle Eyes spoke to him softly, "do not be afraid for these braves have been sent by the Great Spirits to show you the error of your ways. Listen to what they have to say. They have travelled here to help you". A very old chief stepped forward. He told the brave "the hatred that you carry is burning away at your heart. Unless you stop carrying this hatred around with you it will destroy you". At that moment the brave's wife appeared and she asked him to stop fighting and to care for their daughter. She told him "it is bad enough my child has lost her mother do you want her to lose her father as well?" Eagle Eyes looked at the brave and saw the tears running down his face. He knew now that this brave was starting to learn. As quickly as the blue mist appeared so it vanished, leaving the three of them in silence around the fire. Eagle Eyes asked the brave "tell me what you feel from your heart not what you think from head". After a while the brave turned to Eagle Eyes and said "the visions I have seen here have made me realise the path I have been travelling will lead to my destruction unless I change my ways". He stood up and walked over to where his daughter was sleeping and gently picked her up and cradled her in his arms. Tears ran down his face as he then held her high above his head and shouted, "Great Spirits hear me. I will do everything in my power to change my vengeful ways. This I swear on my daughter's life". He then made a promise to his wife that he would always be there for their daughter. At that moment one single crack sounded and one flash of white light broke up the black darkness of the night sky. Eagle Eyes stood up and walked over to the brave and placed his hand on his shoulder. He told him "Be at peace my friend, the Great Spirits have accepted your promise. Now rest for you will need your strength for the journey ahead".

As daylight started to break through the darkness Eagle Eyes felt an overwhelming feeling of peace and tranquillity sweep over his entire body. Even he had learnt something from that nights' experience.

The following days ran into weeks and then into months. Time flew by and all the time their number was growing until the day finally arrived when Eagle Eyes realised he had gathered all his people together. There was only one thing left to do and that was to lead them home. He rode his pony up a steep slope overlooking the valley where they were all camped for the night. The black darkness was lit up by small fires dotted everywhere as far as the eye could see. As he gazed down at his people he felt proud. He could feel the trust and the hopes of the Indian people run through his entire body. At that moment he realised that all the Indian people were standing up and gazing at him. He did not understand why until he heard the voice. A voice he knew well. It was his friend The Warrior. As he turned around The Warrior and White Spirit were stood there, White Spirit still as magnificent as ever. The Warrior told Eagle Eyes his journey was nearly over and he should feel proud for he had achieved something very sacred. He had brought different tribes together to form one Indian nation. "This task you have carried out was virtually impossible but you have achieved it through sheer determination, faith and the will to bring our people together as one. A nation proud of its past but more importantly its future". Eagle Eyes told The Warrior, "I did wonder why the Indian people were standing there gazing up – they can see you and White Spirit!" The Warrior told Eagle Eyes "There is only one figure they can see and that is you. The Great Spirits have placed a white glow around you and your pony. The Indian people see this as a sign from the Great Spirits and this is why they stand – to give thanks to the Great Spirits above for sending you to lead them to the Promised Land". He told Eagle Eyes Starlight and her child were well and tears ran down Eagle Eyes' face at the mention of her name. The Warrior placed his hand on Eagle Eyes shoulder and told him that in a few moons they would be together and would not be parted again. He also told Eagle Eyes that he would have to perform one more task – to protect his people before they reached the Promised Land. The Warrior told Eagle Eyes, "When this task becomes a reality think from your heart and the task will be resolved. In three moons you will be faced with the biggest challenge of your life. The only advice I can give you is to listen to the drums, they will provide you with the answer you seek". Eagle Eyes turned to The Warrior to ask him what he meant but he was gone. The only thing he could hear fading into the distance were the words of

The Warrior, "listen to the drums, slow beat caution, fast beat action" and then there was silence.He mounted Running Wind and slowly made his way back down to where his people were camped. All that nights The Warrior's words kept running through his head and as dawn approached Eagle Eyes prepared his people for the last part of their journey. He told them that whatever lay ahead they must not be afraid for he would lead them to the special place and that no harm would come to anyone as long as they listened to him and followed his directions. The people were silent and Eagle Eyes could sense their fear. He told them "whatever happens you must all stay behind me. Do not panic and most of all do not move". Eagle Eyes mounted his pony and proceeded onward and the people followed.

The dust cloud from so many people on the move could be seen for miles. Eagle Eyes, aware of this, glanced upward. There flying high in the sky was his eyes. Scanning the horizon for any sign of movement the eagle flew high and low calling out as he soared through the air. Eagle Eyes knew the eagle would let him know if any danger lay ahead.

The next two days passed without any sign of danger. That night as they all camped, Eagle Eyes knew that the following day would bring the conflict The Warrior had warned him about. He continuously rode up and down talking to the people, reassuring them that although when dawn broke there would be danger lurking on the horizon they were not to be afraid, "you must all stay behind me and whatever happens you must not move for the Great Spirits will watch over you". That night Eagle Eyes did not sleep. He kept wondering what he would face and how he would react. At that moment his pony started pounding his front legs, rearing up and down. Eagle Eyes got up and went over to his faithfully friend and placing his hands around the pony's nose he whispered in its ear, "its alright my friend, whatever lays ahead we face together". The pony shook his head up and down then stood silent. Eagle Eyes patted him on the side of his neck and returned to the fire. Dawn was approaching and the light of day was starting to break through the darkness of the night. The Indian people were up early that morning, perhaps they could sense the urgency of the events that were about to take place. Eagle Eyes could sense the restlessness in his people and he again rode up and down trying to bring a sense of calmness. He kept telling his people "remember what I have told you, stay calm and do not move. The Great Spirits will protect you from whatever may lay ahead".He then started to lead his people onwards towards their promised land. A land of peace and tranquillity, far away from the slaughter and starvation of the reservation areas his people had been held captive in. They had been moving for about four hours and were crossing a high ravine surrounded by high pointed rocks, ahead high in the sky, Eagle Eyes could see the eagle. He was circling high some distance ahead. Eagle Eyes carried on for about another hour then stopped for his people to rest. Eagle Eyes took a drink from his water bag, slid from his pony's back and poured some water into a bowl and held it while his pony drank. He then remounted the pony and just sat there watching. He knew something was about to happen, he could feel it. All the time his eyes were scanning the horizon for any sign of danger but there was only silence. He knew he had to get his people to the high ledge by nightfall because when the sun started to rise it would show the opening in the rocks. Once through the mountain his people would be safe and in the land he had promised them, but he also knew that to get to the high ledge they would have to cross an open plain and this was the area where the conflict would take place. He started to lead his people onward again and after only an hour they reached the point where the ledge started to dip downward towards the grassy open plain. Eagle Eyes knew something was wrong. No birds were singing and the only thing moving was the long grass swaying in the light breeze. At that moment the eagle's cry could be heard. Eagle Eyes glanced upward. Just a short distance away the magnificent bird was circling frantically, soaring high and then low. Eagle Eyes knew this was the place. He told his people to stop and not move. A group of braves begged Eagle Eyes to let them go with him but Eagle Eyes told them to stay. He told them, "What ever may lay ahead, whatever you may hear, do not move, wait until I return". As he slowly moved away from his people he glanced back for just a moment. He could see the fear on their faces. He stopped and turned Running Wind around and spoke to his people, "do not be afraid for no harm would come to you and you have my promise I will return". Eagle Eyes turned back slowly. He started to move forward, slowly at first, and then Running Wind began to increase the pace. Eagle Eyes could feel the wind's light breeze on his face. Strange thoughts were going through his mind. Feelings of fear, feelings of not wanting to let his people down, after everything that had happened they had been through enough. Whatever lay ahead had to end here. He knew that his people would be watching, he also knew that if he did not do this right he would lose his people forever. This was a price he was not prepared to pay, he had come too far for that.

As he and Running Wind got out onto the vast grassy plain they were met by cannon fire. Explosions were going off either side of them, enormous pieces of stone, grass, mud and tumbleweed were being blown high up into the air, pieces landing all around them. Eagle Eyes stopped his pony. He could not see anything for the dust was so thick in the air. All he could hear was the sound of stone and mud hitting the ground. It was then that he heard the drums beating slowly. He knew he had to proceed with caution. As he moved slowly through the thick dust cloud he could see the faces of past Indian chiefs. They were all saying the same thing to Eagle Eyes "be ready to act for the lives of your people lay in your hands. The courage and the strength you need have been given to you. Do not be afraid to use it". As the dust started to clear Eagle Eyes was confronted by a sight he would never forget. Ahead of him were about four or five hundred soldiers and there in front of them were six cannon pointing directly at him and his people. As he started to move forward the cannons started firing again. Eagle Eyes and his pony vanished in the thick dust cloud. Cannon after cannon fired at the same spot. All his people could see were fragments of earth being blown high in the sky. They could not see Eagle Eyes or his pony. They thought surely he was dead but they waited patiently for what seemed like an eternity until eventually the cannons stopped firing and the dust cloud started to clear. The sight that met their eyes was unbelievable. First they saw an outline surrounded by a bright white light. The outline got brighter and brighter and eventually they could see it was Eagle Eyes and Running Wind. The pony was stood up on his back legs, his front hooves pounding the air in fury. It was not only his people who were amazed. The soldiers could not understand either. Why, with all the cannon fire directed at him, was he still alive? Running Wind's hooves eventually dropped to the ground and he slowly started to move forward. Eagle Eyes could hear the drums beating faster and he knew now that this was the time to act. As he got closer to the soldiers they began to fire their guns at him. He stopped and raised his hands into the air and flashes of bright blue light came from his fingertips. One soldier raised his rifle and aimed it directly at Eagle Eyes. Eagle Eyes directed the blue light towards the soldier and within second the soldier was engulfed in the light. As Eagle Eyes lowered his hands the soldier fell silently to the ground. Other soldiers rushed to his side but it was too late, he was dead. Eagle Eyes called out for the officer in charge to step forward. There was silence but eventually an officer stepped forward. He stood tall on his horse, the sabre in his hand glinting brightly in the sunlight. He told Eagle Eyes that he had been sent to take his people back to the reservation. Eagle Eyes waiting until the officer had finished talking. When Eagle Eyes started talking his words were not only heard by the soldiers they were heard by his people as well. The words carried on the light breeze gently blowing across the grassy open plain. Eagle Eyes asked the officer, "Have you not had enough of killing? How many more of my people's blood has to be spilt to satisfy your lust for vengeance?" The army officer just starred at him. He told Eagle Eyes, "My orders are to take these people back to the reservation where they belong". Eagle Eyes looked at the officer and said, "My people are free and deserve the right to live in peace. Generations of my people have roamed this land long before the white man came. Then these plains were covered with buffalo and antelope and we only killed for food. The skins we used for clothing and moccasins. We lived in harmony with nature. This was our way until the white man arrived and killed all the buffalo, not for food, but for greed. He worked against nature, killing everything in sight. The white man carries so much hatred. He is motivated only by power and greed. He then turned his attention to the Indian, stealing their lands, killing and driving them away, forcing them to exist on nothing. We are not animals. We will not be forced into pens you call reservations. You call us savages because we have fought back. We fight to survive! Our whole existence depends on it! If the white man has his way we will be wiped from this earth". He looked the officer straight in the eye and said, "That day will never come. We were here before you and we will be here long after you are gone". The army officer raised his sabre into the air. Eagle Eyes raised his right hand and directed his power at the officer's sabre. It was engulfed in a bright white light and within seconds he dropped it to the ground. The sabre glowed bright red as it burnt the grass around it. As it settled on the ground Eagle Eyes told the officer, "You may have many soldiers and many guns but the power that comes through me is far more powerful than yours. There is no need for anyone to die here today. Let my people pass in peace and no harm will come to you". The army officer laughed out loud, so did his soldiers. Eagle Eyes and Running Wind moved backwards slowly. Eagle Eyes could hear the drums beating rapidly and he knew the time for talking was over. He raised both arms in the air. Bolts of blue light flashed from his hands and headed high into the sky. Within seconds a massive black cloud formed high above, lightening bolts flashed through the blackness of the cloud. White flashes of light lit the outer edges of the cloud and as he moved his arms across the sky the massive cloud moved with them till it hung directly over the soldiers. With tears in his eyes Eagle Eyes lowered his arms and as he did so the massive blackness engulfed the soldiers below. Screams and cries could be heard but all that could be seen was blackness and flashes of blue light passing through the darkness. After a short time the massive ring of darkness started to disperse. As it faded it slowly revealed a picture of death. Bodies lying motionless on the ground, soldiers lying slumped over their horses. Only one soldier remained standing and unhurt. The army officer stood just looking but saying nothing. Eagle Eyes and Running Wind moved closer. Eagle Eyes got off his pony and slowly walked over to the officer standing alone amongst his dead soldiers. He told him, "You were given the chance to let my people pass in peace yet you chose the path of destruction. You have been sparred today to return to your people and tell them what you have seen. There are no marks or wounds on any of your soldiers. Their spirits have been released from their bodies of torment by the Great Spirits who have taken them to a place free of greed and killing". The army officer looked at Eagle Eyes with tears in his eyes but was filled with too much emotion to say anything. Eagle Eyes mounted Running Wind and slowly moved away to rejoin his people.

Eagle Eyes and his people moved slowly passed. None of them would ever forget what had taken place or the sight of that lone soldier surrounded by so much death. That night they made camp on the high plain overlooking the mountains, awaiting the sunrise that would reveal the opening in the mountain wall and the last part of their journey. Eagle Eyes sat alone that night reflecting on the day's events. He felt sad but relieved. He also thought about Starlight. It had been many moons since they had been together and yet it seemed the time had passed so quickly. In a few short hours they would be together. As he sat there he felt a hand on his shoulder and heard a voice he knew well. It was his old friend The Warrior. They talked about what had happened and The Warrior told Eagle Eyes that what had taken place was not of his doing. Eagle Eyes told The Warrior that he had never seen so many bodies in one day before and that he had hoped for a peaceful solution. The Warrior told him, "You did your best. You gave the officer the chance, he chose to ignore you and from then on it was out of your hands. The Great Spirits released those souls from their tormented bodies, at least now they are free". He told Eagle Eyes that he and the Great Spirits were proud of him. He had completed his quest and within hours he and his people would be safe and free. The Warrior stayed with Eagle Eyes until just before the sun started to rise and then he was gone. Eagle Eyes gathered his people and together they awaited the dawn. As the sun started to rise its rays bounced off the two peaks of the mountain beaming down a ray of light that showed the opening in the mountainside. Eagle Eyes began to lead his people one last time towards the opening and as they reached it he waited on Running Wind while his people entered. Once inside flaming torches lit the way. It took hours before finally Eagle Eyes entered the opening. He followed the last of his people through the vast corridor of rock until eventually it opened out onto the beautiful grassland. His people were home.

Eagle Eyes gazed around looking for Starlight but with so many people gathered he could not see her but eventually he heard her voice crying out to him. He turned around and there, standing with her young son in her arms, was Starlight, still as beautiful as he remembered. He slid from his pony and embraced them. Tears ran down Starlight's face as she held them both. Eagle Eyes glanced upward as he heard The Warrior's voice saying, "Rest now my friend for you are home and at peace. Embrace your family for now your work is done".

Chapter 6

The Battle

Eagle Eyes and Starlight sat by the fire talking. Apart from them the only other sounds to be heard were the branches on the fire crackling, small flakes of wood glowing red, so light they floated silently up into the darkness and the crickets singing their nightly song. Eagle Eyes put his arm around Starlight's shoulder and kissed her gently on the cheek. Starlight reached out and held Eagle Eyes' hand. She gazed into his eyes and told him that she had never been so happy. He pulled her close and gently kissed her on the lips. At that moment Starlight's son arrived on his pony. He truly had grown into a fine young warrior. He spoke to his mother and then sat by Eagle Eyes, talking of his adventures that had taken place that day. He told him how he had followed a deer and had gotten really close to watch the mother feeding her young one. Eagle Eyes mind was taken back to a time when he too was a young brave being shown the old ways by his father. Now time had passed and it was his turn to show his son the old Indian ways. But Eagle Eyes knew these were not the only tasks he would have to learn for this young warrior would carry on in Eagle Eyes' footsteps when it was his turn to join the Great Spirits above. Starlight looked at Eagle Eyes but said nothing. Eagle Eyes knew the time was fast approaching when he would have to leave his family once again in search of his people. He felt troubled inside. His whole body wrenched with sadness but deep down inside he knew he had to go on one last journey to gather as many of his people as he could and bring them back to this land of tranquillity and peace. He knew that Starlight felt this overwhelming sadness as well.

That night Eagle Eyes went off alone. He knew that before daylight dawned he would see his old friend the Warrior and between them his path would be shown. As he silently moved through the grassland an owl hooted. Eagle Eyes glanced upward, the old owl was perched high up on a branch. Eagle Eyes paused for a moment and wondered what this old bird knew and what would lie ahead. After about an hour Eagles Eyes stopped by a slow running stream. He knelt down by the edge and drank. The water was cold yet the taste was very sweet. He sat there, the moonlight reflected in the slow running water. The shimmering movements of the moon were also reflected by the small rocks as the water ran over the tops of them. The air was full of fragrance with the perfume from the flowers that lay all around. Apart from the owl occasionally hooting the night was still and quiet. Eagle Eyes gazed up at the night sky. Stars were shining bright, their night-glow standing out brightly in the blanket of darkness. He knew in his heart that this was a very special place. Shortly after he had the feeling that he was not alone. As he glanced around he saw his old friends the Warrior and White Spirit slowly walking towards him. The Warrior spoke to Eagle Eyes telling him he was sorry for coming to him again but that there was no other way. He told Eagle Eyes that he felt his sadness and pain and Eagle Eyes slowly placed his hand on the Warrior's lips. He told him, "I understand why you have both come to see me. I have been expecting you". The Warrior embraced Eagle Eyes, tears flowing down his face. As the three of them sat talking it was as if they had never been apart. The Warrior told Eagle Eyes of the suffering of his people. How they had been forced off their lands by the white man's greed. He told him, "Many have died of starvation, many have been killed by the white man and many have been forced to flee in search of food but were caught and returned to the reservation, penned up like animals". He told Eagle Eyes that when the moon has shown itself for the third time he would have to leave. He told him how sorry he was for disrupting his life but that he would have to go for he was the only one who could save their people. White Spirit sat there, his penetrating blue eyes staring straight ahead. Eagle Eyes placed his hand on the magnificent creature's head. The wolf never moved. Eagle Eyes turned to the Warrior and said, "To think many moons ago I was frightened to do this. I have learnt so much and yet I understand so little". The Warrior smiled. He told Eagle Eyes, "You have a wise head full of knowledge. Just trust in your beliefs. I and White Spirit will watch over you, you have nothing to fear. The Great Spirits will give you all the help you require to complete your final task". Eagle Eyes stared at the Warrior for a moment but before he could speak the Warrior told him again not to worry, "you will return to your family, no harm will come to you". Eagle Eyes said to him, "I should have known you already knew was I was thinking before I said anything". The Warrior placed his hand on Eagle Eyes' shoulder and told him, "Go back to your family old friend. Spend as much time as you can with your wife and son. Make sure they feel special, tell them it is them that you will be coming home to when this final task is over". The Warrior stood up and so did White Spirit and they moved slowly away and disappeared into a swirling blue mist. It was only the Warriors words that could be heard being carried gently on the night breeze telling Eagle Eyes that he was not alone. Then he heard White Spirit howling out his cry. He knew then that it would be no easy task, for White Spirit only howled in times of suffering and pain or before battle.

Eagle Eyes returned to his family. Starlight was waiting for him and she threw her arms around Eagle Eyes and started to cry. She told him she was frightened, she had heard a wolf howling in the distance. Eagle Eyes held her tightly and told her not to worry. He told her, "The wolf you heard is a friend, you have nothing to fear from him. He is our protector and will guide us through any troubled times". She held on to Eagle Eyes tightly as they disappeared inside their tepee. That night she held onto him so tightly that it was difficult for him to sleep, he just lay beside her watching her sleep and wondering how many moons would pass before he would see her face again.

The next two moons passed so quickly they seemed to be gone in a flash. Eagle Eyes knew that the next moon would signal his departure from this peaceful place. That day Starlight was very quiet. She hardly said a word and as the day started to draw to an end Eagle Eyes found her washing some clothes in the nearby stream. He stood there for quite a while just watching as she squeezed the water from the clothes and then rubbed them continuously on the rocks trying to remove any stains or marks. Tears ran down her face yet she made no sound. As Eagle Eyes approached her she turned around, wiping away the tears from her eyes. He reached out and tenderly held her in his arms, his right hand stroking her long black hair. He whispered softly in her ear that he loved her and told her that while he was away she would be watched over by the Great Spirits above. He placed her hand upon his chest and asked her what she felt. She told him, "Your heart beats like a drum". He told her "My heart beats for life, the blood that pumps through my body will give me the courage, the air that I breath will give me the energy I need to complete my task". He told her, "Any time you feel lonely or sad think about my heart beat, that alone will take away your sadness and fill your body with happiness. All the things we have done together will coming flooding back to you, putting back that wonderful smile on such a beautiful face". She held him tightly and told him, "I know you have to go but every moment you are away from me will be an eternity". Still holding her, her gently kissed her and said, "Come help me prepare my things", and as they walked slowly beck to their tepee Running Wind appeared on the horizon. Starlight looked at Eagle Eyes but before she could say anything Eagle Eyes said, "There is a sing. My faithfully friend is eager to start our journey. He has come to find me. The time for me to go is very near". Starlight prepared some turkey meat and a water bag and Eagle Eyes placed his blanket on Running Winds back. At that moment Starlight's son appeared. He walked towards Eagle Eyes, tears flowing down his face, and they embraced each other. Eagle Eyes told him, "While I am away take good care of your mother. You are the head of this family until my return". Eagle Eyes asked him to hold out his right hand and as he did so Eagle Eyes pulled out his knife and made a cut across the boy's palm and then his own. They gripped each other's hand tightly, blood dripping slowly from their union. Eagle Eyes told him, "My power and courage now flows freely through your body. When I take my hand away your wound will be healed" and as they released their grip a look of amazement shone from the boys eyes. As he looked at his hand, which showed no sign of injury, Eagle Eyes smiled at him. He then took hold of Running Wind's mane and jumped onto his back. He looked at Starlight and her son, smiled, said farewell and disappeared over the hill. He reappeared for a few seconds, waved, and vanished into the night.

After about an hour he reached the passageway leading through the mountain. As he entered the torches lit one by one illuminating his way through the darkness. Running Wind began to gather pace, the noise from his hooves ricocheting around the walls of the mountain. Eventually Running Winds pace began to slow, it was as if he sensed the opening to the mountain was near. As they emerged Eagle Eyes glanced back. He could see the torches going out one by one, returning the passageway to total darkness. He gazed up at the sky and although it was still dark he could see the stars twinkling. The moon's glow lit up the valley casting its brightness across the open grassland. Wolves could be heard howling in the distance as he rode on. Just before daybreak he stopped and made a small fire, took a drink from his water bag and ate some turkey meat. Running Wind grazed on the lush grass, moistened by the early morning dew. As the sun started to come up Eagle Eyes could feel its warmth as it rose higher. White fluffy clouds floated motionless in the pale blue background of the sky, birds sang their morning song and a light breeze blew across the vast plain. Occasionally tumbleweed was caught by the light wind and it would be pushed across the plain. Eagle Eyes sat taking in all the sounds, his long hair brushing the side of his face as the breeze grew stronger and then weaker. He knew this was nature's way of telling him that changes were about to take place. He mounted Running Wind and carried on his journey. He rode all that day. As the sun started to go down he made camp by a couple of big old trees. As darkness fell he sat by the fire, its red glow standing out in the darkness, tiny flakes of glowing wood being gently lifted upwards. He gazed constantly at the fire as if it had some kind of mystical power but all he could see was Starlight's face smiling back at him. At that moment he heard a twig snap and turned around to see his old friends the Warrior and White Spirit walking towards him. The Warrior spoke to Eagle Eyes, "We have come old friend. We thought you needed some company". As the two of them sat talking White Spirit kept pacing around and around. The Warrior asked White Spirit to sit with them and eventually he stopped and sat opposite them. Eagle Eyes turned to the Warrior and said, "My people are close, I can feel their presence". The Warrior told Eagle Eyes, "This is why White Spirit is restless. He can sense them as well". The Warrior also told Eagle Eyes that his battle would start just after daybreak. He told him he would hear gunfire and when he reached the top of a ridge he would see for himself the mass slaughter of his people. His task would be to save as many as he could. He told Eagle Eyes, "You will feel many emotions but through all of this and what ever happens you must stay focused on your people. All you need to take with you is your lance, this alone will defeat the white man for the power of the Great Spirits will flow freely through it. You will direct its power and you alone will be the white man's downfall and destruction". At that moment the Warrior stood up. He placed his hand on Eagle Eyes shoulder and said, "Farewell my friend". He and White Spirit walked slowly away disappearing into a blue mist. Eagle Eyes sat there wondering what would greet him at daybreak. Thoughts of his people's suffering brought tears flowing down his face. At that moment the Warriors words could be heard carried on the night breeze, "Do not worry my friend for I will be with you and White Spirit to help guide you through whatever lays ahead. Rest now for daybreak is nearly upon us and you will need all your strength for the battle that lays ahead". It was not long before daylight started to break through the darkness and Eagle Eyes started packing away his few belongings. He put out the fire that had kept him warm through the night. He slowly walked over to where Running Wind was standing and gently placed his blanket on the pony's back. He gently stroked the forehead of his old friend who moved his head up and down briskly while stamping his right hoof constantly on the ground. Eagle Eyes knew his old friend could sense danger ahead. He glanced around one last time to make sure he had left nothing behind. He picked up his lance, jumped on Running Wind's back and rode slowly away. He had not been riding long before he heard the terrifying sound of canon and gunfire. He knew that by the time he reached the top of the ridge that many of his people would already be dead. Running Wind began to gain pace; it was as if he knew that every second counted. Once they reached the top Eagle Eyes stopped Running Wind. He could not believe the mass slaughter he was witnessing. His people were being cut to pieces by cavalry soldiers who were swinging their sabres cutting arms, heads and legs off defenceless women and children and when they retreated his people were being blown to pieces by canon fire. Tears ran uncontrollably down Eagle Eyes face. Rage and hatred raced through his body. Running Wind reared up onto his hind legs. A light wind blew Eagle Eye's hair across the side of his face. He raised his lance to the sky above. As he lowered the lance he moved it slowly across the where his people were, slowly moving its point across from side to side. He then moved the lance slowly away from his people and directed it above where the soldiers were. As he and Running Wind raced towards them Eagle Eyes started his war cry. The sky above the soldiers turned black, lightning bolts shot towards the ground striking the metal barriers of the canons making them glow red in the darkness. Lightning continued to rain down on the soldiers below. Their cries could be heard, their bodies could be seen being hurled into the air, illuminated by the blue lightning. Time after time the lightning bolts rained down on the soldiers below, scorching the earth with its immense power. It was then that Eagle Eyes noticed he was not alone, there were three warriors on either side of him, all silhouetted in a blue white light and with their lances pointed towards the soldiers. He glanced down, Running Wind's hooves were moving very fast yet they were not touching the ground. It was as if he was being carried along, yet how could that be as dust clouds were following behind them. As Eagle Eyes got closer to the soldiers the warriors on either side of him started to disappear. One by one they vanished as quickly as they had appeared. Eagle Eyes pulled gently on Running Wind's reigns, bringing him to a halt. As he sat there he looked around him. There were bodies everywhere, some still burning. Yet amongst all this death one lone figure stood silently. It was the commanding officer that had given the order for his men to attack Eagle Eye's people. Eagle Eyes moved slowly towards the silent figure. He stopped running Wind and slid from his back. He then stood for a moment looking at the silent figure surrounded by death. Eagle Eye's asked him, "Does this satisfy you? All your men are dead because of your hatred towards my people. The white man has killed my people, driven them from their land! Why have your people got so much hatred towards us? We were on this earth many moons before you". The officer looked at Eagle Eyes but said nothing. Eagle Eyes told him, "Your people are driven by greed, you take everything this land can give but you give nothing back". It was then that the soldier raised his sabre in the air and started running towards Eagle Eyes, shouting, "savages". Eagle Eyes shouted at him to stop but he still kept running towards him. Eagle Eyes raised his lance and threw it towards the oncoming soldier. As it struck him he dropped his sabre. He dropped slowly to the ground, both his hands clutching the lance. In his last moments of life he looked at Eagle Eyes but said nothing. Eagle Eyes grasped the lance and pulled it from the soldier's body and at that moment the blackness lifted and the brightness o the day returned. As Eagle Eyes looked around him all he could see were burned bodies of soldiers scattered around, the stench of death and burning flesh filled his nostrils. This was a sight he would never forget. At that moment he noticed some of his people taking clothing and possessions from the dead soldier's bodies. He shouted to them to "stop and gather together away from this place of death". His people sank to their knees, praising him for defeating the soldiers. He told them all to stand up. He told them, "It was not I who defeated the soldiers but the Great Spirits above. I have been sent to lead you to a land of peace and away from the white man's greed. Tend to your own dead and injured. I will return to you when the moon is high, but do not enter this place of death while I am away. You must build platforms for the dead so they can start their journey to the Great Spirits above. When you have done this you must wait silently for my return but heed my warning, any person entering this place of death will not live, for the Great Spirits will destroy anyone or anything that enters this place of death except the vultures who are the cleaners of the Mother Earth. What ever remains after will be claimed back by her. The white man took everything and gave nothing but at least in death he is giving something back". His people stood silently as Eagle Eyes mounted Running Wind. Before he slowly rode away he turned to his people and said, "Remember what I have told you, those who enter this place will feel the anger of the Great Spirits. There has been enough killing here today, do not let there be any more" and with those last words spoken Eagle Eyes rode away. He rode swiftly, his long hair floating in the breeze, images of the battle constantly going through his mind. He felt an overwhelming sadness. Never before had he seen such a waste of human life. Questions ran through his mind: if the Great Spirits could control life and death then why had they allowed this to happen? Why did they let his people suffer? He could understand why they had intervened and why they had destroyed the soldiers, but in his mind he wondered if there was another way to have avoided all this suffering? Eventually he stopped. He rubbed down Running Wind with his blanket, placed both his hands around his faithful friend's head and whispered in his ear "Thank you". His old friend moved his head up and down as if in acknowledgement.

Eagle Eyes walked over to a tall tree that stood proudly on its own, its branches reaching high up into the sky. He sat down, closed his eyes and began to chant. He sat there for quite some time until he was aware of a presence. He heard nothing yet he sensed he was not alone. He slowly opened his eyes and there sat in front of him were his old friends the Warrior and White Spirit. The warrior held out his hand to Eagle Eyes who grasped it frantically, tears running down his face. The Warrior told him that what had taken place was the will of the Great Spirits. He told him that although the sadness he felt weighed heavy on his heart he must think of all the suffering his people had endured. The brutal killings and starvation, being forced from the land their ancestors had roamed for generations. He told Eagle Eyes that he and the Great Spirits were very proud of him. He also told him not to be sad, for those soldiers who had died had chosen their lives, they had also chosen when to die. He told him, "I know you question the actions of the Great Spirits, they know this and that is why I come to you now, to explain their actions. When you went into battle you felt anger and hatred. You wanted to destroy the white man for all the suffering he has inflicted on our people. The feelings you felt are human, they were not given to you by the Great Spirits. These are feelings deeply embedded in you". He also told him, "Until the time comes when man can live with man in peace these battles will continue. The Great Spirits know this and this is why they chose you to lead their people on this earth, away from the white man's destruction". Eagle Eyes grasped the Warriors hand firmly. The Warrior told Eagle Eyes, "Your journey is nearly over. All that awaits you now is to lead your people home. Your wife and son await your arrival. They too have missed you". The Warrior rose to his feet and told Eagle Eyes, "Rest now my friend for in a short while the day's brightness will be here and it will be time for you to return to your people and lead them home". As he and White Spirit walked slowly away he turned to Eagle Eyes and said, "You can call upon me and White Spirit anytime and we will both come to you when we are needed". He also told him "When you start to lead your people away, place your lance over the battle ground and move it gently from side to side. All that happened there will dissolve into the Mother Earth and the valley will be restored to a grassy plain", and with those last few words he and White Spirit were gone.

As Eagle Eyes mounted Running Wind to begin his journey back to his people he had an overwhelming feeling of peace run through his entire body. He knew deep inside that what had happened was for a reason and the decisions taken were made by a presence more powerful than him. As darkness fell he reached the top of the hill leading down to the valley where his people were waiting. He could see the burial fires ablaze as he slowly rode towards his people. When he reached them they were stood around silently. He told them to gather their possessions and to make sure the injured were tended to for at first light they would start their final journey home. As Eagle Eyes glanced up at the night sky, the moon shining brightly, he noticed a shooting star twinkling as it moved swiftly across the blanket of darkness. He knew this was a sign from his old friend that daylight was approaching. Shortly after daylight started to break through the blackness of the night and as the sun started to rise Eagle Eyes gathered his people together for the start of their final journey. As they moved off Eagle Eyes stopped and told them to wait. He rode over to the battle place and looked at all the remains of bodies lying on the ground. He raised his lance, gently moving it from side to side over the entire area. As he did this, a white mist covered the battle area and as he moved his lance back the mist disappeared leaving just the grassy plain in view. Everything connected to the battle that had taken place was gone, the land had returned to its natural state. Eagle Eyes glanced at his people who were waiting for him in silence. He said nothing. He returned to them and they rode slowly away. No words were spoken.

After three days travelling they reached the top of the ravine leading down to the mountain where at daybreak the sun would reveal the opening that would lead them all to a land of peace and tranquillity. Eagle Eyes told his people to rest for in a few hours they would be home. They looked at him but said nothing. He told them, "I know what you are thinking, why have I led you here? All you can see is a mountain! All will be revealed when the sun touches that piece of rock" and he pointed to the big overhanging rock. "It will send a beam of light across to that mountain, revealing an opening which we all will travel through". As the dawn started to break and the sun started to rise, its rays hit the piece of rock and sent a beam of light across revealing the opening through which they all entered. As they travelled deep into the mountain their pathway was lit by torches and as the last person passed each one the torches went out. One by one returning the passageway to darkness. After a few hours the passageway opened out onto a plush green land. Eagle Eyes turned to his people and said, "You are home now. Put up your tepees, live your lives for you have nothing to fear here". He then rode swiftly to his own tepee where he slid off Running Wind's back and ran inside. But Starlight was not there. He walked slowly down to the nearby stream and there he found her washing some clothes. He called to her softly and she turned around. When she saw it was Eagle Eyes she ran to him sobbing. He held her firmly in his arms, kissing her passionately. She told Eagle Eyes that he looked tired but she was glad that he was home. He told her he would never leave her alone again. At that moment their son arrived. He jumped down from his pony and hugged his father. The three of them, arm in arm, walked back to their tepee and disappeared inside knowing they would never be parted again.

Or would they………..

Chapter 7

A Time of Change

The land was peaceful and calm. Eagle Eyes and Starlight walked arm in arm. He looked around him at his people going about their daily tasks, laughing and enjoying life. It was good to see. Eagle Eyes thought back to the time when life was not so easy. Starlight grasped his hand tightly. She knew her husband would never forget those tragic times. They would always be there to haunt him. Eagle Eyes smiled down at her, he knew there were things that he could never tell her. Yet, when he gazed into her eyes nothing else mattered. He knew he would always be there to shield her from harm, not that any danger could befall this beautiful land, after all it was protected by a force far more powerful than him. He thought of his old friend and the beautiful white wolf with the penetrating blue eyes. Many moons had passed since they last talked and Eagle Eyes missed their presence.

That night he went off as he did every night, just walking and thinking. He sat down by an old oak tree standing proudly, its branches reaching up into the darkness. As he gazed upward the stars twinkled brightly in the moon's rays casting shadows on the ground below. He again thought of his old friend. Memories of their talks together flashed through his mind and at times brought a smile to his face. He thought of all the troubled times they had been through together, then he heard a familiar voice asking him if he wanted some company. He turned around slowly and there is front of him stood The Warrior and White Spirit. They hugged each other and White Spirit stood up on his hind legs placing his paws on Eagle Eyes' chest. Eagle Eyes placed his hand on White Spirit's head and said "I have missed you both". The three of them sat and talked, it was like old times. The Warrior sensed his old friend was troubled. He could see the pain in his eyes. The Warrior asked Eagle Eyes "what is troubling you old friend? You are sat with us yet your heart is elsewhere. Tell me my friend what is troubling you". Tears ran down Eagle Eyes' face, his hands trembled. The Warrior clasped his old friend's hands to steady them but it took quite some time for Eagle Eyes to speak. The Warrior had never seen his old friend so upset. Eagle Eyes told The Warrior he had seen visions in his dreams about his beloved Starlight. Visions he could not come to terms with. As he spoke the tears ran more frequently down his face and his hands continued to tremble. The Warrior could sense Eagle Eyes' fear and he asked him "why do you fear death? It is part of life. We all have our journeys to take. None of us know where they will lead us. Each and every one of us is guided by the Great Spirits above. We are shown the paths before us but it is up to us to make the choice of which path we follow. You and Starlight have enjoyed much happiness together. The visions you have seen are to prepare you for Starlight's rise to the Great Spirits above". Eagle Eyes looked at the Warrior, tears running down his face, and said "I do not want to live without her! She is my life!". The Warrior clasped Eagle Eyes hands, "You of all people should know even in death you will not be parted. She will always come to you when you call her name". Eagle Eyes told The Warrior he had noticed Starlight was hardly eating and how frail she had become. The Warrior told Eagle Eyes "she has been holding onto life for you, she knows how hard it is for you to let her go. She knows the time is nearly here for her to rise to the Great Spirits above yet her only thoughts are of you. Stop feeling sorry for yourself and return to her. Show her your love so that she can rise in peace from the worry and pain. You only have two moons left together on this earth, do not waste time. Tell her all the things in your heart, show her the dew on the flowers, listen to the early morning bird song, walk through the long grasses together, hold her in your arms, tell her how much you love her. These things you do will put her mind at peace and will make you come to terms with her passing". He told Eagle Eyes to go to Starlight. He also told him to remember that even in death we are not alone. Eagle Eyes stood up and wiped away the tears but when he opened his eyes his old friend was gone.

Eagle Eyes returned to find Starlight struggling to carry water back to their tepee. He took hold of the water pouches and placed them on the ground. Starlight's hands were bleeding from where the straps had embedded themselves into her hands. Eagle Eyes gently bathed her hands and wrapped some cloth around them to keep the wounds clean. He picked her up in his arms and took her into the tepee. Even though her hands must have been very sore she did not say a word. Eagle Eyes placed her on a blanket. Her frail body looked so lifeless and tears began to flow down his face. Starlight placed both her hands on Eagle Eyes face and wiped away the tears. She told him "do not be sad my husband for I am going to the Great Spirits above. We only have a short time together, let us not waste it on weeping tears. Even though I will be gone I will always be watching over you and our son until we are all together for eternity".

Eagle Eyes held Starlight close, her frail body looked lost in his arms and the tears ran down his face as he could feel the life ebbing away from her body. He held her tightly hoping the moment would never end. He told her how much he loved her and how her love had made him complete. At that moment her eyes opened and she smiled. Eagle Eyes had never seen her look so radiant, she had a reddish colour to her cheeks. She spoke softly to him telling him that meeting him had made her life complete and that no other man made her feel the way he did. He told her to rest but she would not listen. She told him "I must tell you what is in my heart while breath is still in my body. You have brought light into my life where there was darkness, you brought me song when there was silence, these things I will always love you for, you were my strength when I was weak, all these things you must know before the time comes for me to pass". She told Eagle eyes not to be sad. She told him life was just a short passing in time and if you are lucky your life cycle entwines with another. Tears again ran down Eagle Eyes face. Starlight gently wiped them away telling him that even in death they would never be parted and that she would always be there at his side, she would never leave him. He held her tightly in his arms while telling her constantly how much he loved her. Her hands cupped his face gently to her chest all the time he was talking. He did not realise her hands were slipping gently from his face. Starlight had slowly slipped away to the Great Spirits above. Eagle Eyes cried out. You could hear the pain of his loss in his voice. Even the birds stopped singing. The only sound to be heard was Eagle Eyes' sobbing. He held her frail body as he wept and kept talking to her, unaware that their son was standing behind him. He too was crying, after all Starlight was his mother. He placed his hands on his father's shoulders and told him to be strong. He told him "my mother has spoken to me about this time and how I must be strong for my father for this would be the only time that he would show weakness and that it would be me who would stand strong for my father giving him the strength to come to terms with the loss of his beloved wife". Eagles Eyes gripped his son's arm tightly but said nothing as no words needed to be exchanged. They both knew in their hearts the love they felt could never justly be put into words. As they both grieved people arrived and surrounded their tepee. The medicine man chanted, drums beat slowly and they could be heard over many plains. Carried on the winds of time, to be heard by many but not by all. After two moons Eagle Eyes emerged from his tepee, is face torn with sorrow, he said nothing to anybody but walked slowly through the people who moved aside as he made his way up to the place he shared with his beloved Starlight. This is where he would build the wooden platform that would release her spirit to the great ones above. Day and night he worked alone, building the platform on which his beloved Starlight would lay. Finally it was ready. He returned exhausted to his tepee below. There he found his son talking to his mother who lay silent on a blanket of animal fur. Eagle Eyes told his son, "It is now time to release your mother's spirit to the great leaders above. He slowly knelt down and picked up his beloved Starlight. His son followed his father as he slowly made his way to the place where he and Starlight had shared so many happy times. He placed her frail body gently on the platform and covered her with her favourite blanket. He gently kissed her on the forehead one last time and then slowly moved back, allowing their son to speak to his mother and to say to her his final goodbyes. He finally knelt over his mother gently kissing her on the cheek. He then moved back behind his father.

As the light of the day began to fade, Eagle Eyes moved forward towards the platform. Tears ran constantly down his face as he lit the fire which would release his beloved Starlight's spirit. It was not long before the flames engulfed the whole platform, the bright orange glow standing out against the darkness, flames leaping up higher and higher breaking up the darkness of the night sky. Eagle Eyes and his son just stood there paying their last respects, a husband's love for his wife and a son's love for his mother. Both of them stood there all through the night and as daylight broke through the darkness the last small embers of the platform were all that remained. Eagle Eyes and his son stayed there for another two moons before returning to their tepee below. Throughout all this time no words were spoken. Eagle Eyes would never be the same person again. He became withdrawn and would go off alone for many moons, returning as he left in silence. It was as if he was searching for something, yet deep inside himself he knew his beloved Starlight was not far away. He had lost part of his faith. How could the Great Spirits take his beloved Starlight? He had always followed their ways! What had he done to make them so angry to take his beloved Starlight away and leave him to travel these Great Plains alone? This was a question that went through his mind constantly. His son begged his father to talk but Eagle Eyes pushed him away saying only that he needed time to come to terms with the loss of his wife. His son became angry, shouting at his father saying, "She was my mother, I feel the same pain as you, yet since my mother's death you have pushed me away". Eagle Eyes held out his hand but his son said nothing. He moved slowly towards his pony and as he mounted the pony glanced at his father then he rode away into the distance. Eagle Eyes sat there, his head lowered in shame. It was not his son's fault his wife had died yet he had pushed him away when he should have been standing with his son giving him strength, not making him stand alone with his grief! No wonder he rode away! He did not deserve the love of a son whose father had treated him that way!

That night, Eagle Eyes sat alone staring into the fire knowing that he must make things right between himself and his son when he felt a presence with him. This was something he had not felt for a long time. Suddenly he felt a hand on his shoulder and as he turned around he knew it was his old friend The Warrior. As they sat Eagle Eyes talked, yet The Warrior said nothing. After some time The Warrior stood up and Eagle Eyes asked him where he was going. The Warrior told him "at last you have stopped talking about yourself and how you feel. What about your son? Does he not feel the same loss you feel? Your son is out there alone. You should be comforting him, giving him the strength and support to come to terms with the loss of his mother yet you stand here drowning in your own self-pity. Your wife would be ashamed of you to see you in this state. You of all people should know the spirit never dies, it just passes onto another place, a place where self-pity would never be allowed to exist. Ask for guidance and it shall be given. Even now the Great Spirits watch over you, knowing you will return to them. In three moons Starlight will come to you, make sure you have good news for her. Go find your son and lose the bad blood between you", and on those words The Warrior vanished as quickly as he had appeared. Eagle Eyes stood there for a moment reflecting on the words of his old friend. He knew deep inside himself that his old friend, The Warrior, was right. For days he had thought of no one but himself, drowning in his own self-pity when he should have been with his son helping him with the loss of his mother. Eagle Eyes returned to his camp, mounted his pony and went in search of his son, praying to the Great Spirits above for guidance in finding him and hoping he could mend the rift between them.

He rode for two days before he found his son's pony grazing near a stream. His son looked up at him and said "why are you here? When my mother died I thought we would stand together and face our grief but you left me alone to fight this loss which even now I cannot come to terms with". Eagle Eyes ran over to his son and held him tightly. He told him he was sorry for not being by his side and that he hoped his son would forgive him. Tears ran down both their faces as they hugged each other tightly. Eagle Eyes told his son, "In one moon you and I will see a vision. I do not want you to be afraid. You will remain at my side but remember what you see will not harm you. Remember, the Great Spirits above will guide you as they have guided me. When the time comes for me to join your mother it is you who will carry the power of the Great Spirits above". He told his son, "I have taught you many things but you have many more to learn and when you reach your father's age you will still be learning!". Eagle Eyes laughed and placed his hands on his son's shoulders. "Don't look so sad" he said. "It will be a long time yet before I join your mother yet you will see her tonight when the sun's glow fades into darkness. Do not be afraid, this is the Great Spirits wish that you and I talk to her and put her mind at rest. She has seen the way I have treated you. I must apologise to her for not being at your side for she has looked down on us from above and is sad to see a father and son torn apart by grief and sadness. We must put her mind at rest and show her we now stand together. This will be the only thing that will make her happy and at peace". His son held his father's arm tightly. There were no words spoken but they both knew what was in each other's hearts.

That night as darkness fell they sat around the fire watching the flames leap up licking the darkness of the night air, the wood embers glowing and crackling in the darkness. Then, with no warning, a blue mist started to appear, thick yet in places transparent. White light appeared, bright and then sparkled. It seemed to light up the night sky. Without warning the silhouette of a figure appeared in the distance. Eagle Eyes and his son watched as the figure came closer. Eagle Eyes son stood up and called out, "it's my mother". Eagle Eyes stood up and placed his arm around his son's shoulder as if to reassure him and told him not to be afraid. At that moment Starlight stepped out of what seemed to be a swirl of blue and white mist. It outlines her body as she moved forward and placed one hand on Eagle Eyes' face and the other on her son's face. She told them both that she was happy to see them standing together. Eagle Eyes tried to speak but Starlight placed her hand on his lips and said "please be them both, "I have been watching you tear yourselves apart over my death when you should have stood together. My dead should have brought you both closer together yet it only pushed you apart. It broke my heart to watch a father and son be torn apart by grief". She looked at Eagle Eyes and told him, "You should have known better. You know how people react to death yet you allowed yourself to wallow in your own self-pity. Our son is young and has no knowledge of death. All he sees is a person who is no longer breathing, a person who is lifeless. You should have been there for our son yet you chose to go off alone. It took a visit from the Warrior spirit to bring you to your senses. You and I have led a very happy and fulfilling life together yet you chose to let our son face my death alone. I watched as he rode away not understanding why his mother had died and worst of all not understanding why his father had shut him out and gone off alone". Eagle Eyes told Starlight that he knew he had been wrong but that he had not been able to help himself. He held her hands with tears running down his face and at that moment their son shouted "even as a child I never saw you two raise a word against each other, yet now when we have the chance to be together even for a short time you waste it by casting blame. I am not interested in whether my father should have done this or whatever. I am pleased to see my mother. I know my father will always be by my side. Can we please forget the past and enjoy what we have now?" Bother Eagle Eyes and Starlight were silent. They both knew their son has grown into a young man with a good head on his shoulders, a young man whose knowledge would grow and make him into a great leader. They all hugged each other and the three of them talked into the early hours until Starlight stood up and said "come here my son". She kissed him gently then she turned to Eagle Eyes and kissed him too. She promised them both that she would return and her last words to them were "look after each other" then she disappeared in a cloud of swirling blue mist as quickly as she had appeared.

Eagle Eyes and his son sat looking at each other, happy yet sad, contented yet knowing that there would always be a part of their hearts that would never heal, a part that would always remain empty, a part that could never be filled. For Eagle Eyes the physical loss of his wife would always leave an empty space in his life. For their son the loss of his mother would always leave an emptiness inside his which could never be filled. Although he knew his mother was watching over him he missed her closeness and guiding hand. At that moment he heard his mother's voice whisper softly in his ear "I will always be here for you my son, ask for my help and it will be given". He smiled and raised his eyes above, for he knew deep inside that his mother would never desert him.

The two of them mounted their ponies and rode slowly away. The sky started to darken and in the distance lightning flashes illuminated the horizon and feint cracks of thunder could be heard. Eagle Eyes told his son, "The earth is being quenched of her thirst, heavy rains are falling which will bring new growth to the land. We must find shelter before the storm reaches us". They rode on until they reached a small canyon where protruding rocks reached out and underneath a small cave went back far enough to give them shelter from the storm. Eagle Eyes told his son to bring the ponies inside as the lightning would frighten them. He built a fire and as they sat around it the flames illuminated their faces. By now it was dark yet the night sky was lit by blue and white flashes and the sound of Mother Nature cracking her whip could be heard as the rain pounded on the rocks above. Feint wolf cries could be heard in the distance as Eagle Eyes and his son talked through the night. This was a special time for the two of them. They had not been this close since his son was very small. It felt good.

The rain stopped as the daylight started breaking through bringing a new day. Birds were singing as they looked out over the canyon under the deep blue sky with white fluffy clouds floated endlessly by. Mother Earth had provided for them that night. Eagle Eyes put out the last remaining embers of the fire and they led their ponies out of the cave and left.

Eventually they came upon a small rock pool which had been formed by the rain the night before. They washed their faces and breathed in the sweet morning air. Eagle Eyes turned to his son and said, "This is what life is really about. The freedom to roam these plains without fear. One day, when all evil has been driven from these lands, our people will once again work in harmony with Mother Earth to try and restore the balance. Only then will peace and harmony be returned". His son said nothing but he knew what his father was saying. His father had told him many time of the destruction and greed the white man had inflicted upon his people. He had seen the torment and horror in his father's eyes. Like his father, his main aim in life was now the survival of his people. Like his father, he would not stand by and watch his people be wiped from this earth. Eagle Eyes turned to his son and placed his hand on his shoulder. He told him, "we have the ability to speak but no words are being spoken yet I know what you are thinking and are about to say. You also can do this. Look deep into my eyes and you can read my thoughts before they are spoken. This is a gift from the Spirits above. Look after it well my son for you will use it many times in your lifetime". He looked deep into his father's face. He had not notice before the deep lines of life carved there. Eagle Eyes smiled at his son "Do not worry" he said, "these lines all mark special times in my life. Old age does not come alone my son, it always leaves its mark upon a face". "You are not old" he told his father, "you are just a wearer of time". Eagle Eyes smiled and put his arm around his son's shoulder and told him, "There will be times when you will not believe what you see, there will also be times when what you are hearing will be beyond belief. All these things I tell you from my heart are true. A father's love for his children can never be matched, the bond we share is very special and this makes us as one being. In the eyes of Spirit we will always be as one spirit in search of peace and the preservation of our people. We will never be wiped from these lands, too much of our people's blood has soaked into this earth. One day the truth about the horrors our people have suffered will be told. Only then will all of our warriors spirits will be released to roam these lands again". His son placed his hand on his shoulder, no words were spoken yet they both knew what was in each other's heart. They rode off in silence yet they were in conversation without the sound of words.

As darkness fell they made camp. As the fire crackled and the red embers floated up into the darkness, Eagle Eyes told his son to get some sleep as they had a long day ahead of them. His son wished him goodnight and wrapped his blanket around himself. Eagle Eyes sat counting his blessings as he watched his son sleeping. He knew he was a true warrior in the making. Experience and guidance were the only things left for Eagle Eyes to teach him. He truly had grown into a young warrior and was gaining knowledge every day. Eagle Eyes knew his own time was coming to an end and one day he would hand over everything to his son. He gazed out into the darkness where the outline of the mountains was lit by the moon, its shimmering light cascading over its ledges. Eagle Eyes stretched out by the fire, gazing up at the moon's brightness, before he fell asleep.

As morning broke he was awakened by the sound of the birds singing in the sunlight. He sat up and looked over to his son who was still sleeping peacefully. Tears of joy yet sadness ran down his face. He was sorry he would have to leave his son yet he was happy in the knowledge that his son would cope with what ever faced him in the future. He and his mother could always give him guidance from above, after all, the Spirits had forecast this moment. There will always be new beginnings but all life must give way in the end, passing to a higher, better place. Eagle Eyes knew his time was coming to an end. He was becoming frail as everyday passed. He had been visited by his wife,

Starlight, who had told him she would be there to help him pass over peacefully. His old friend The Warrior and the wolf had also visited him, talking to him and reassuring him that it would be his turn shortly to join the Great Spirits above and enjoy a long rest. He wanted to stay and as he gazed at his son he knew he had to make the best of the little time he had left. His son opened his eyes and asked his father what was wrong. Eagle Eyes said there was nothing wrong but his son then asked "then why are tears running down your face?" Eagle Eyes replied "My son these are tears of joy not tears of sadness. Come, let us go, we are wasting valuable time". Eagle Eyes put out the last embers of the fire before he mounted his pony. He gazed upward. He wanted more time but he knew this was not possible. Looking at his son he knew he had to make the most of what ever time was left. As they rode over the vast plains they talked. This was a good time and Eagle Eyes felt blessed with a sense of belonging and pride. He knew time was slowly slipping away from him. His son looked at him and asked if he was alright and Eagle Eyes replied, "I am fine but a little tired. These days I find I just do not have the energy I used to. I am getting old. It will not be long now my son before you will have to carry on for me". Eagle Eyes son said "please father, don't talk like that. We will rest here. After a good night's sleep I am sure you will feel a lot better". Eagle Eyes got off his pony and sat down, wrapping his blanket around his frail old bones. His son fetched some wood and made a fire. It was starting to get dark and the wolves could be heard howling in the distance, the wind rustled through the branches of the trees. Eagle Eyes told his son "there is a storm coming". "But the night is still – a little wind maybe" he replied. Eagle Eyes told him "When you have lived as long as me you can sense changes. It may appear calm now but before this night is over rain, wind and lightning will be cast over this land bringing new life to the earth. His son smiled at Eagle Eyes, "how can you know this?" Eagle Eyes looked into his son's eyes and replied "I have been on this earth a long time and in that time I have learnt many things. You will learn that in a life time many changes happen. There are things you can control but there are many things that you cannot. There will be many happy times but there will also be many sad times. This is life my son. You have to learn to adapt, bend with the wind, if you are in the river go with the flow of the current. If you do not Mother Nature will sweep you to one side. You have these gifts installed in you. When life gets tough reach within yourself and you will find the courage you need to overcome these situations, but remember also that your mother and I will always watch over you. You are protected by the great Spirits above. You have nothing to fear. You will be guided every step of the way. Just follow your inner spirit, it will not let you down". As they talked the rain started to fall, the night sky lit up by lightning flashes, each one stronger than the last, the thunder crashing through the darkness, blue light illuminating the hills and landscape in the distance. As they sheltered from the rain under their blankets Eagle Eyes son turned to his father and said, "How did you know?" Eagle Eyes stretched out his hand and placed it on his shoulder. "Experience, my son. This will come to you in time. You will be able to predict the changes of Mother Earth but never take her for granted! You must live in harmony with her. Remember, she can give you everything but she can also take everything away. Mother Nature has no master and answers to no one".

The following morning they woke to the bird's morning song. Eagle Eyes got to his feet slowly. The cold and wet of the night had got deep into his frail old bones. His son helped him get onto his pony and as they set off Eagle Eyes knew this would be the last day he would have with his son and tears ran down his face. When his son saw his tears he asked him what was wrong and Eagle Eyes replied "nothing my son. I am just glad to be with you on this glorious bright day". His son asked, "Father, are you in pain? I see your tears yet you say nothing is wrong." Eagle Eyes replied "tears come with old age my son. When you get to my age you will understand what I mean". As they rode across a small stream they came across an old tree which had been split in two, its fine old branches laid out upon the ground. Eagle Eyes stopped and said to his son "Look, what do you see? His son said, "An old tree lying on the ground. It has fallen because it is old". Eagle Eyes looked at his son and said "Your eyes are open but you do not see what is before you. It was the storm that brought down this old tree, not old age. Look at the branches, they are scorched. Mother Nature's power brought this old tree crashing down. Never doubt her power my son, for remember she shows no mercy. This old tree was standing here many moons before I was born but now it is its turn to make way for new life. New growth will start and the life cycle will start all over again. Many moons from now another strong old tree will stand here, her branches reaching up to the Spirits above". Eagle Eyes sat down, he was feeling very tired. His son placed a blanket around his shoulders and gave him water from his bag. As he sipped the water slowly, Eagle Eyes asked his son to sit with him. Quietly he told him "it is time". His son said nothing, tears filling his eyes. He grasped Eagle Eyes hand tightly and Eagle Eyes looked at his son and smiled. At that moment he slowly fell towards his son and silently drifted away. His son cried out but there was nothing he could do. His father had departed to the Great Spirits above.

For quite some time he sat holding his father in his arms, tears streaming down his face. He knew what he had to do. He laid his father out on the ground and wrapped him in his blanket. He then collected wood from the fallen tree and built the platform where he could release his father's spirit. He gently laid his body on the platform and followed his father's instructions to the end. By now the light was starting to fade and with tears flowing uncontrollably down his face, he set the platform alight. It was not long before the flames took hold, engulfing the whole platform. Crackling wood and red embers lit up the darkness. The flames rose for most of the night but as daylight approached just a few small flames were left burning the few remnants that were left.

He looked around to where is father's pony had been standing with his while he was building the platform, but then he remembered what his father had said to him many times. "Don't look for my pony for she will be with me. I will need her to travel to the Great Spirits above". He gazed upward and heard his father's voice "Leave now my son, for your work here is done. I am with your mother now and we will both be watching over you. The Great Spirits send you their blessing".

With that, Eagle Eyes' son mounted his pony and slowly rode away, knowing that he must carry on his father's work, putting his people first and fulfilling the quest which was now placed upon him by the Great Spirits above.

This book is a result of me being persuaded to visit a spiritualist church with my wife and sister. It was there that I met the Revs. Joy and Roger Wood who introduced me to a psychic artist named Patrick Andrews. During our conversation he drew a sketch of a Red Indian Chief called Lone Wolf and told me that he was my spirit guide. Up to that point, as your average every day lorry driver, I had no urge to write a book of any kind but shortly after I began to experience an overwhelming urge to write. I didn't know what; I just knew I had to write something. This is where my journey started. Shortly after I joined a meditation circle and I started to see pictures in my head of an Indian brave sat on a pony overlooking an Indian village. The urge to write got stronger and eventually I asked my wife to buy me a pad and some pencils – just to try. Words seemed to flow from my pencil but I had no idea what I had written until I read it back and as time went by I felt strongly that these words couldn't have come just from my imagination. My belief is that they have been given to me by my spirit guide Lone Wolf in the hope that they will be passed on to other ordinary people like myself and maybe give hope for a better world. The Journey is about a Red Indian warrior who returns to his village to find that everyone, including his wife and son, have been massacred. It tells of the hate and torment he feels after burying each and every one of them. He is then visited by the Great Spirits who give him the courage and vision to carry on and discover an inner peace which he uses to complete his given quest to help show mankind that they can live together if only they would listen and learn by remembering the way things were.

Stephen Simmons

www.ingramcontent.com/pod-product-compliance
Lightning Source LLC
Chambersburg PA
CBHW051305250626
47155CB00009B/3445